ALONG FOR
THE RIDE

MIMI GRACE

Copyright © 2019 by Mimi Grace

Print Edition ISBN: 978-1-9991082-1-2
Cover design and illustration by Leni Kauffman
Editors: Christa Soulé Désir and Johanie Martinez-Cools

Content Notes

These brief notes are for readers who need some insight into the contents of this novel. Some may view the following as spoilers.

- Deceased parent (dies long before the start of the book)
- Verbally pushy person interested in the heroine (NOT the hero)
- Several sexually explicit scenes

Chapter 1

JOLENE BAXTER SUSPECTED she was some sort of masochist who enjoyed the special hell where avoidable inconveniences dwelled. She was wide awake on a Saturday morning without coffee, standing in front of her sister's recently sold house studying the massive moving truck she would operate on a sixteen-hour trek across the country. Adding to her agitation and restlessness was the thought of making the journey with the one person she would rather never spend that many uninterrupted hours with.

"Thank you so much for doing this," Jolene's older sister, Nicole, said as she exited her almost empty house. She offered Jolene a travel mug that held coffee. Nicole wrapped her arms around her sister's shoulders.

"You know I love you, but if you think I'm not going to steal that gorgeous rug that was in your bedroom for compensation, you're deluded."

"Oh, shut up," Nicole said as she flicked Jolene's ear. "You wouldn't dare."

"I wasn't going to do it initially, but because of recent

developments"—she shrugged—"I'm actually considering it."

"You know I would've tried to pick someone else to go with you if it weren't last minute," Nicole said as if that sensible explanation would help Jolene not feel anxious and annoyed about her trip with the arrogant and cocky Jason Akana.

She stifled her desire to complain about him. She tried to be as nonchalant about the whole situation as possible. Think person-in-a-tampon-commercial-spinning-in-a-cornfield laid-back. But nothing said, "I'm totally unbothered" like changing travel outfits multiple times and settling on a less comfortable but more visually appealing jeans-and-light-sweater combo. Jolene ignored that these particular jeans had become a little tight in the last few months and would most likely give her issues on the long trip.

"I'm sorry Dad bailed," Nicole said after a moment.

"If I got a free trip for two to the Bahamas, I would also forget I had daughters. Besides, I told you, I'm taking the rug as compensation."

Nicole rolled her eyes and replied, "Fair enough, but I know there's tension between you and Jason, and I don't want you to be miserable during the entire trip…or catch a homicide charge."

Fortifying her resolve not to complain about the less-than-ideal circumstances, Jolene said, "Seriously, Nicky, don't worry about it. First, Auntie Julie is a fantastic criminal defense lawyer. Second, I'll simply rotate between FaceTiming you and Mom. She can put down her sangria to relieve me of a hellish trip for a few minutes."

"I can't believe I'll be a sixteen-hour drive away from you," her sister said, abruptly changing topics.

Jolene shook her fist at the sky. "Damn being a brilliant

and talented architect who gets amazing opportunities at prestigious companies far, far away."

Despite her best efforts, Jolene's voice caught on the last few words. Her sister embraced her once more. Jolene refused to cry because her sister deserved good things, and she wouldn't make it any harder for Nicky by crying about being more than a fifteen-minute drive away. Jolene had jumped at the chance to help her sister and brother-in-law move across the country, partly because they were family and she would do anything for them, but also because the trip would work as Jolene's mea culpa for regularly being difficult and at times complicating her sister's life.

"Do you ladies want some of these muffins?" Nicole's husband, Ty, asked as he joined the women on the driveway, interrupting what would've been an ugly cry session. The tiny apron he wore looked comical on his large body made for playing full-contact sports. His big smile exposed all his straight white teeth.

"No!" both women shouted too quickly.

Jolene didn't need any of her brother-in-law's concoctions he called food to further complicate her trip.

"C'mon, try a tiny bite," Ty encouraged while he pressed a muffin to his wife's lips.

"Ty, baby, I'm not going to eat the science experiment you made from the remaining products in our pantry," his wife said.

"Jolene, how about you take some for the journey? They're not that bad," he said.

Jolene let out a grunt. "Do you remember Mom's sixty-first birthday party?"

The two women burst out laughing at the memory of their mother, Jacqueline Baxter, sputtering and spitting out the disgusting tart Ty had baked for her. She hadn't had time to grab a napkin before the reflex to get rid of the taste hit. Their mom embodied the refined Black church lady, and her subsequent conclusion that her daughter's new husband had tried to poison her had been absolutely distressing.

"Hey, man," Ty shouted, his voice cutting through the women's laughter.

Jason had arrived undetected in an Uber, and made his way across the street to Nicole and Ty's recently sold house. The laughter died down, and Jolene forced herself not to react unnaturally to Jason's sudden presence. The arrogant tilt of his head tempted Jolene to roll her eyes and suck her teeth. But in a demonstration of her herculean control, she pasted a saccharine smile on her face instead. Jason ate up the distance between them with large strides and sure footing. His straight black hair dared not move out of place despite sufficient winds and what looked like a lack of hair product. The morning sunlight played with the golden undertones in his brown skin, a blessing from his Polynesian heritage.

Her smile faltered a bit when he finally arrived before her. They stood closer than they had in years, and she must've forgotten his arresting eyes and how tall he was. He all but towered over her, and she had the urge to take a healthy step backwards. She'd last seen him at Ty and Nicole's New Year's Eve party. They hadn't greeted one another, and they never found themselves in the same room.

Jason hugged Ty in that way many guys hug, with a lot of patting and thumping on each other's backs, then he gave her sister a gentle squeeze, but Jolene only received a simple nod. She quelled an odd feeling that sprung at the dismissal.

"See, Jojo? He only has a backpack, so your suitcase

will definitely fit in the front." Nicole pointed to the bag slung over one of Jason's impressively broad shoulders.

"It's barely a two-day trip," Jason said while he stared right at Jolene. His brow slightly furrowed.

"I needed a large suitcase for the wardrobe changes every five miles," she retorted.

"Then in that case"—he gave her a quick once-over —"I hope to be impressed."

She wasn't quite sure if he made a judgment on her current outfit or the body underneath that would hypothetically be exposed in this ridiculous set-up. The possibility of the latter made her sweat. His eyes met hers again, and everyone—including Jason—waited for her to say something snarky. She failed to come up with anything and instead buckled under the intensity of his brown eyes. Thankfully, her lovely sister could sense she was drowning and interrupted the silence, which had gone on just long enough to make things uncomfortable, with a quick airy laugh.

"Why doesn't Ty give you both a tour of the truck, then Jason can come inside and pick up the coffee I have for you in the kitchen," Nicole said before she walked back into the house.

Ty slid the back door of the box truck open to reveal its contents. "In here we have most of the furniture and appliances from our bedroom, living room, and kitchen," he said, motioning toward the extremely packed interior of the van.

Jolene spotted the rug she so admired wedged between a mattress and the van's wall.

"Don't worry about driving any differently, the fragile stuff is in our car," Ty continued.

Ty and Nicole planned to leave several hours after Jolene and Jason because they expected the buyer of one of their personal vehicles to arrive later from out of town. The passenger area of the moving van had two seats and very little space between them. A small suitcase would definitely make the area feel more squished.

"What's your number?" Jason asked as the three of them made their way to the house after the tour.

Under any other circumstance, Jolene might've been thrilled or at least slightly satisfied that an attractive man had asked for her number. But he delivered the question so matter-of-factly and without the slightest hint of flirtation that she recited her number like she would while ordering a pizza. A few moments later, a message came through her phone.

"I've set up a driving schedule and possible pit stops we'll take on our trip," he said.

Jolene studied the detailed itinerary that outlined how Jason would take the first six-hour driving shift and they'd swap places after lunch. He'd written out the gas stations they'd stop at and the possible restaurants and fast-food chains they might be interested in. He even included their operating hours. She now remembered how particular he was. Firmly pressing her lips together, she battled another rise of annoyance. She ultimately lost the internal fight and didn't thank him for the perfect itinerary or even give an appreciative smile.

Instead, Jolene looked at him and said, "Wow, you really know how to take the fun out of things, don't you?"

Jason winced, and Ty stifled a laugh.

Jolene Baxter would get on his last damn nerve on this trip. Jason had hoped, thought, and even prayed that she might not be the same obnoxious and immature twenty-three-year-old woman he met five years ago at Ty's wedding. But when he got out of the Uber and her boisterous laugh pierced the otherwise serene street, he suspected the next two days would try him.

There wouldn't be any peace with someone who purposely antagonized people. His only connection to Jolene was through Nicole and Ty, and thankfully that limited their interactions to a few times in a given year. She looked a little curvier from when he last saw her, and her black hair, which he'd only ever seen straight, was now really curly and piled on top of her head in some sort of bun. He'd always found her attractive, but whatever appeal her curves and smile had were eclipsed by an aggravating personality.

When they entered the house, Jolene collected her bag while Jason found the travel mug Nicole had promised in the kitchen. As Jason sipped his coffee, Ty wrapped up muffins in napkins on the kitchen counter.

"Man, you have to take some muffins for the road," Ty said.

Jason looked at the rocklike objects skeptically. During their time at dental school, Ty had been legendary for his horrible baking. Most of their friends had indulged Ty in his attempts till they got sick from what he made.

Jason shook his head. "I got a ton of food. My mom packed some leftovers for me when I had dinner at her place last night."

"You can't have too much food," Ty said while he stuffed the two napkin-wrapped muffins into the side pocket of Jason's backpack that miraculously held everything. "How's your mom doing, by the way?"

"She's good. She started a podcast with my aunt, and they're honestly living their best retiree lives," Jason said while he mentally planned where along the trip he would dispose of the muffins.

"Seriously? That's awesome. I need to find something interesting like that to suggest to my parents."

"Yeah, it's great because they're so busy with that and their other social commitments that they don't have enough time to worry about me."

"Well, I appreciate you taking time to help me move my stuff."

Ty was his best friend, and if he was being honest, his only real friend. Ty had refused to let him be the loner that came naturally to him during orientation week at dental school almost a decade ago. They'd gone through school together and created a bond that left Jason willing to do anything for him.

"It's no problem, man. I've never driven this trip, so it'll be interesting."

"Oh, the landscapes and terrain are the least interesting thing you'll have to contend with," Ty said.

"We should be heading out now if we're going by *your* schedule," Jolene said as she entered the kitchen. Her mini suitcase trailed behind her on the tile floor, and her high-pitched voice echoed through the empty room.

Jason was sure somewhere a mirror fractured. Ty folded his arms across his beefy chest and grinned. Jason gritted his teeth and gave Jolene a complying nod. When one of your good friends asked you to accompany his sister-in-law across the country last minute, you did it with as much grace and composure as you could muster.

Chapter 2

THEY'D BEEN on the road for a few hours and other than when Jolene pointed out the mountain goats an hour outside of the city, they'd not said anything to one another. Jason glanced over to Jolene once in a while to see what she was doing. And for hours at this point, Jolene had taken to tapping and clicking away at her phone and scribbling things in several notebooks she had sprawled across her lap.

It surprised him that the trip seemed to be unfolding pleasantly. There was no unnecessary chatter, the music he enjoyed played, and he drove with a passenger he wouldn't even notice if not for her distractingly delicious mango-and-coconut scent.

A ringing sound disrupted the stasis they'd settled into, and Jolene turned the music off and held her cell phone to her ear.

"Hi, Yvonne. I got Christine's email and it's a go," Jolene said, tapping Jason's shoulder and motioning for him to roll his window up. "No, use the silver one instead of the black one," she continued. "But put it inside and not around the back of the display, it looks tacky and cluttered when you can see the cords."

The bizarre conversation went on for another five minutes and when she finally hung up, it became clear to him that he actually didn't know what Jolene did for work. He knew that she'd gone to college but didn't know the specifics. The assertive way she had spoken on the phone was messing with his previous idea of her. He supposed she might be more mature than he thought.

Before he could reconsider, he asked, "What do you do?" He cringed inwardly, knowing he had just broken their unspoken agreement to remain silent.

She looked at him for a long moment, and he thought she might ignore his question. But then she said, "I'm an account manager at Able & Quinn. It's a public relations agency that specializes in beauty, fashion, and lifestyle brands."

He nodded. Intrigued, but trying to close the dam he'd unintentionally opened. He didn't want to give her the impression he wanted to talk. He turned the music back on.

"It's hard, and not as glamorous as people think," she continued over the noise, "but it's such a beautiful thing when you complete a successful campaign or launch a brand to great reception." She looked at him quickly. "One day it'll be cool to have my own firm."

He had to force himself not to moan out loud that she was still speaking. By the way she talked about her work, he could tell it excited her because her arms moved dramatically while she spoke. She looked like a bird trying to take flight for the first time. Her enthusiasm was charming. It briefly reminded him why five years ago he'd almost asked her out. But again, he didn't want to chat, because he was convinced their silence was keeping the animosity at bay.

"What current project are you working on?" he asked, surprised to realize the question had come from his mouth.

Motioning toward the paper and notebook cocoon she had created around herself, she said, "Right now we're in the thick of things trying to launch this apothecary line. The clients are a little difficult, but we're on schedule for a late-summer launch party. We begin a mini press tour in a month or so. It's the biggest account I've ever led."

Jolene knew she was rambling. From the start of their trip, they'd travelled in silence as if entombed in a library, and she'd just driven a sledgehammer into it. Later on, she'd reflect on how needy and pathetic she seemed, like an uncoordinated kid at a tap dance recital looking at the audience for approval. But it thrilled her to flex her accomplishments to Jason. She would rather chew glass than admit it, but she wanted him to be impressed by her skills, because he was a successful dentist who graduated from a prestigious dental school.

She'd worked really hard to shed the funk that came with graduating high school a year late. Her sister had been the brilliant one who'd soared through her undergraduate with plans to complete her Master of Architect degree. Jolene, on the other hand, when she finally stumbled her way into college, had to work incredibly hard to make decent grades. College came with a steep learning curve. Skipping classes in high school and doing the bare minimum hadn't prepared her for the hard work and responsibility to come. Naturally, she battled feeling inadequate.

But pleasure had bloomed in her chest when she'd looked at Jason and caught his mild interest. It had encouraged her so much that she blurted out how she wanted to own her own PR firm one day. A dream she let simmer in the back of her mind. No one, not even her closest friends or family, knew about it. But she resented the idea of him seeing her as she was years ago. She was worthy of him having an actual conversation with; she was no longer a hot mess.

However, Jason's polite smile and less than enthusiastic response to her rambling worked as a cold dose of reality, and Jolene recommitted herself to their pact of silence. He'd never been talkative anyway, even when they were on speaking terms. Unfortunately, in that moment the electric voice of James Brown filled the small confines of the vehicle.

"Ah, I love James Brown," she said as she turned the volume up.

Jason's music choice till this point had been okay. She bided her time till her turn arrived to put on her own music, but James Brown had been her grandma's favorite artist, so he had a special place in her heart. Jason gave her a sidelong look before they both let the rhythm and funk of "Papa's Got A Brand New Bag" take them.

The desire to go full out and swing her head back and forth nagged, but she would leave that to her solo bedroom concerts. Instead, she tamely bobbed her head and slapped her thigh like she played the tambourine. He drummed his fingers against the steering wheel, which drew her attention to his hands. They looked large and strong. He probably had a girlfriend who appreciated those long, solid fingers. She tensed at the thought of the woman's good fortune.

Obviously, it's been too long if I'm feeling some type of way about a guy I don't even like, fingering a woman I don't even know.

"I remember watching his live performance at the

Super Bowl on TV," he finally said as the song went into its final verse.

"God, how old are you?" She immediately regretted how churlish it came off.

"I turn thirty-six in September."

"That wasn't supposed to come out so harsh or meant to offend, by the way." After a beat she added, "I respect my elders."

That gained her a laugh from Jason. Not a good-natured laugh, but one that was more air than sound. "Don't worry about it, you'll get here soon enough, and when you're older, you're not going to get a pass on your attitude."

"What attitude? I think I'm quite sweet," she said, picking imaginary lint from her lap.

"Are you? I don't think I'd ever describe you as sweet. Perhaps snarky, sarcastic, abrasive, funny even, but not ever 'honey-rainbow-sunshine sweet.'"

"We don't spend nearly enough time together for you to make such a judgment call." She clenched her hands into almost painful fists.

"It's not even noon yet, and you've already called me boring and old," he countered.

"Well, in terms of boring, you're not exactly proving me wrong with your great conversational skills, and as for old"—she gave his slightly gray hair at his temples a pointed look—"I would recommend box color four, dark brown."

If Jolene allowed herself to be honest, she would admit she found his graying hair extremely attractive and dignified.

"The people around you have to inspire the conversation, and honestly, Jolene, a white wall is more encouraging."

"You've called me worse. I'll take my victories where I can," she said.

Jason gave her a look as if contemplating his next words. "You're referring to our confrontation at your parents' place. If I remember correctly, you acted spoiled, immature, and selfish." He shrugged. "I don't know how else to describe getting absolutely wasted at your own sister's wedding and nearly destroying the entire event."

The familiar feeling of shame gripped Jolene's stomach. It humiliated her to watch the videos of her climbing on the wedding party's table and shouting about her misgivings about love and relationships and lamenting about her embarrassingly short marriage at twenty years old. But after copious amounts of wine and several Jäger bombs, her manifesto had been more wailing and cursing than any coherent argument. The incident had caused tension between Jolene and Nicky for a few months. And even long after things had smoothed out between the sisters, guilt gnawed at Jolene.

The day after Nicole and Ty's wedding, however, Jason had thrown salt in the wound. Close friends and family had congregated at the Baxter girls' childhood home for lunch and to open the wedding gifts. Jolene had been nursing a wicked headache and humiliation, but she'd approached the day with a pasted-on smile like she often did when faced with the consequences of her screwups.

Most of the attendees at the intimate gathering had ignored her or given her quick, disapproving glances. When Jason arrived, he apparently hadn't received the memo that operation "ignore the drunk from last night" was in full effect. When Jolene had made a comment about an ugly gift under her breath while Jason stood close by, he had turned to her and scowled.

They'd built a rapport throughout the wedding-planning process, and she found him intelligent and incredibly attractive. At that moment, the disgust she saw in the depth of his eyes had taken her aback. She hadn't said anything overly rude; besides, he'd been the only one who'd caught it. She rolled her eyes and continued to watch her sister and new brother-in-law open their gifts. But her response to his disapproval seemed to annoy him further.

He had stepped close, and in a low voice he'd said, "If I were you, I'd make my presence as low-key as possible."

As a twenty-three-year-old woman almost done with her stint in college, she wouldn't let a man she'd just met a few months ago treat her like some child. "I'm grown. I don't need you to tell me what I should or should not do, thanks."

"You might be an adult, but you're also a spoiled brat. You disrupted my best friend's day, not to mention your sister's. And for what? To make yourself feel special and compensate for your shit personality?"

They'd been standing in her parents' modest-sized living room with a dozen people, but their conversation had thus far gone unnoticed.

"Fuck you," Jolene had hissed.

She might have continued on and told Jason where he could stick his condescending and paternalistic crap if her voice hadn't carried. The previously buzzing room fell quiet. And the weary look on her sister's face as she sat surrounded by half-opened gifts, brought the embarrassment Jolene had fought with the aggression of a baby rhino to the forefront. The weight of it crushed her, and Jolene had made a promise to herself at that moment never to fuck up that badly again. She'd left soon after, and that had been the last time she'd had a conversation with Jason, until now.

———

Jason regretted his intensity the minute Jolene had fallen silent. He knew she hadn't made the comments about his age and demeanor maliciously. He hadn't even been offended, but he saw the opening to push her a little, and he did, and now her face looked gray and solemn. He ran his hand through his hair.

So much for grace and composure.

"Listen, I'm sorry. I don't regret what I said to you back then, because it was the truth, but you're right in saying that I don't know you well enough to make any assessment on your character."

"Don't backtrack now, Jason Akana," she said. The warmth returned to her face as she left her deep thoughts.

The way she said his name made him feel a little tight in his chest. She enunciated the consonants and rolled over the vowels leisurely and made them sound rich and decadent.

Resisting the urge to ask her to say his full name again, he took a couple of measured breaths. "This trip doesn't have to be the place where we hash out our issues with one another or even attempt to convince each other that we're not what the other thinks we are. We're doing a favor for people we care for. That's it."

"Fair enough," she said, giving him a small nod that he read as a sort of truce.

Slowly, as the minutes went by, they returned to a place where comfortable silence reigned. Jolene abandoned the work she'd been doing to stare outside the window at the mountainous landscape with trees that didn't look any bigger than toothpicks.

After a while he said, "There's a gas station we'll stop

at in forty-five minutes. You can stretch your legs, use the washroom, and grab some food if you want."

The scenery transformed from open highway to a rural one-lane road with dense trees lining either side. Eventually they spotted a clearing with a lone gas station. It only had two pump stations and a small convenience store beside it. They found one person already filling gas while two other men sat on a bench right next to the entrance of the store. They all looked up when Jolene and Jason parked their van beside the vacant pump. A long, uncomfortable staring contest ensued that wouldn't let up. Jason got the sense that if either he or Jolene made one wrong move or comment, they'd have a confrontation on their hands.

"How much do you want to bet we're the first people of color they've seen in a while?" she asked, almost whispering.

"Wait, you think they've noticed us?"

She gave him a look full of amusement and disbelief.

"I do have a sense of humor, you know," he said.

"I wouldn't have guessed. You seem like the type who only really watches documentaries that convince you to stop eating meat and gluten."

He rolled his eyes, and they exited the van. The men's gazes remained trained on both of them, and Jason abandoned his initial plan to fill the gas while Jolene went into the store alone. He walked around the van and came to Jolene's side, and they entered the cramped store together. A radio behind the front counter played at an inaudible level, and the heat that had built up throughout the morning made the confined space feel stuffy. The store attendant, a tall man with a wispy comb-over, said nothing. Jason could feel his eyes following them as they maneuvered between the shelves. Jolene picked up for herself a fizzy drink, a large bottle of water, a bag of potato chips, and a couple tabloid magazines. He knew he had snacks from home in his backpack, so he simply purchased a pack of gum.

"I got this," he said.

She looked like she might protest or at least say something smart, but all she did was smile.

"You can go use the washroom as I pay for these," he said, pointing to the door at the back of the store.

She looked at him. "No, I'm fine."

He frowned and started to mention how he wouldn't stop again for a few hours, but she gently placed her hand on his forearm. The contact surprised him, and it stung like an electric current had run through him. Their usual interactions never consisted of physical touch, and he remained quiet, picking up and understanding her silent message. They left the store with their purchased items, and Jason filled the gas tank while the watchful audience kept him company. He knew someone who hadn't been in similar situations would say he imagined the tension. Thankfully, within five minutes, they'd left. Neither one of them said anything until they couldn't see the gas station in the rearview mirror.

"God, I got such a creepy vibe in that store. I just wanted to get out of there," she finally said and let out a big sigh.

Jason nodded. He'd been uneasy too.

"Like, did you see the gun just propped up behind him?" she asked, turning to him.

He shook his head. He hadn't, but her actions and demeanor back at the store now made more sense, and he would've had a similar reaction.

"We're good now," he said, resisting the urge to pat her leg in comfort. "We'll stop in another hour or so for a bathroom break, and you can grab some real food."

He turned to her to make sure the plan suited her, and she smiled at him in a way she'd never done before, full and genuine.

He looked away immediately.

"Oh, 'real food'? For your information potato chips and pop are vital food groups," she said, raising the two items while doing some off-tune interpretation of angelic vocalization.

Jason ignored how suddenly the sound of her voice didn't make him think of shattered mirrors at all.

Chapter 3

"You're sure you don't want any more?" Jolene asked, tipping the half-empty potato chip bag.

Jason shook his head. They'd parked in a lot near a strip mall to eat lunch. It looked like quite the schoolyard lunch set-up. Jason had taken some of her chips, then he'd offered her a granola bar from the full lunchbox he'd brought on the trip. He held up the muffins Ty had baked for them in mock offering.

"God bless Ty, but I'd have to be stranded and starving to eat those," Jolene said.

The doors were ajar, but the pathetic breeze didn't alleviate the heat that had come as the sun reached its peak. Jolene regretted her choice to wear jeans and quelled the desire to unbutton them. She engaged in small talk to distract herself from the heat.

"I can't believe you packed food." Jolene nodded toward Jason's now-empty lunchbox that somehow fit into his backpack full of clothes.

He gave her a look and she swore she saw him smile.

"My mom packed my food for this trip."

"No, she did not." Jolene let out a small laugh. She tossed the evidence of her lunch in the nearby trashcan and got into the driver's seat that Jason had vacated.

"She did. She was a single mom who worked a lot, so I grew up eating fast food until I was old enough to cook. But now that she's retired, she compensates by throwing all the home-cooked meals my way," he said.

Jolene smiled sincerely. "That's precious."

"She's great, the best person I know."

Jolene wondered about Jason's demeanor and personality as a child. She could see him being the kind of kid who'd let the teachers know that recess had technically been over for two minutes. But she could also see him as the child on the playground who stood up to a bully regardless of size. The last visual made her heart squeeze a little.

"Your mother must be proud that you became a dentist."

"My mom and aunt wore traditional Tongan clothes to the graduation ceremony and could barely contain themselves," he said. "It made everything worth it."

Jolene assumed "everything" meant the student loans, studying, and stress. He sounded reflective and a bit distant as he looked out of his window. The momentary silence allowed Jolene to locate vital mechanisms in the unfamiliar vehicle.

"I can drive for a few more hours, if you want," Jason said after some time.

How long had he been watching her? She was mildly annoyed with herself that he detected her nervousness.

"No, it's fine." She turned the key, bringing the van to life. "I can do it."

They'd planned to drive the entire journey without stopping overnight, but it meant they'd arrive at Ty and

Nicole's new home at two a.m. local time on Sunday. It worked because both Jolene and Jason had flights booked for Sunday afternoon to make it back home in time to rest and prep for the new workweek.

With a bravado she didn't feel, Jolene cranked up the air conditioner, turned on her music playlist, and fidgeted with the GPS before maneuvering them out of the parking lot. To her credit, she didn't destroy any of the parked cars. In her mind she gave herself a pat on the back. She looked over at Jason and noticed the unnatural grip he had on his seat.

"Jolene, eyes on the road."

A sarcastic response died on her lips when she immediately drove over a speed bump too fast. She sent an apologetic glance Jason's way. She wasn't a bad driver. Perhaps she gripped the steering wheel too tight and sat too forward, but she was simply a nervous driver. It was a result of never going through Driver's Ed and waiting to get her license.

However, Jolene would have confidently and boldly driven them off the road if Jason had opened his mouth to say something rude about her skills. Perhaps he knew that, because he didn't say a word for a long time.

He finally broke the silence when they hit the freeway. "Are you close to yours?"

"What?"

"Close to your mother, your parents."

"I wasn't an easy child to rear. I was a super sassy teenager, if you can believe it."

He snorted.

"But they're no longer the people who refused to let me get a tattoo at sixteen, so I genuinely love hanging out with them now."

"What tattoo did you want?"

She pressed her lips together and looked at him. "A dolphin. On my ankle."

He smirked as if he predicted her answer.

"Do you have any now?" he asked, and she felt him study her.

She squirmed in her seat and willed herself to keep the vehicle moving in a straight line. "No, I never thought of anything worthwhile after that. You?"

"Just my traditional Tongan tattoo on my shoulder and arm."

"I would love to see it."

"And here I thought it would be *you* removing your clothes in this van," he said.

This time she couldn't stop from swerving. Jason's arm shot out to steady the wheel, and she could sense the maddening smirk on his lips. She fell right into that one. Jolene studied him in her periphery and decided she actually didn't mind talking to him when he held back on the self-righteous act.

———

In and out of sleep, Jason heard Jolene singing off-key. After watching the way she'd nearly swiped a car's bumper as they left the parking lot, his adrenaline levels had dropped enough for him to take a nap once they'd hit straight road. It couldn't have been more than an hour when Jolene's frantic slaps to his arm lurched him back into consciousness.

"Jason, I think something's wrong."

Still disoriented, he straightened in his seat and looked toward Jolene. The first thing he comprehended was how pretty her profile looked, her lips full and pouty and her curls framing her face delicately. It wasn't until Jolene turned panicked eyes on to him that he registered how slowly they moved and the distinct smell of smoke.

"Stop the van and get out now!"

The sun remained unrelenting, and when they exited the air-conditioned truck, the heat enveloped him in its uncomfortable embrace.

"What did you do?" he asked as they both stood in front of the box truck, looking at the large white clouds of smoke rising from the front panel.

She turned to him with her hands on her hips. "What did I do? Nothing."

"Before drifting off to sleep everything was fine, but I wake up an hour later to the truck pretty much on fire," he argued.

She gave him a murderous look. "You actually slept for almost three hours. I felt the truck rumbling, but I thought it was a furniture piece that got dislodged in the back. Then the smoke came. But I *didn't* do anything to bring it on."

"Except not wake me up when you first heard the rumbling."

Through clenched teeth, Jolene said, "I told you. I thought it was furniture moving inside the back." She took a deep breath in. "Instead of blaming me for this, we should probably call for help."

Jason took his phone from his jean pocket and dialed the road side assistance number he'd programmed in his phone. The call dropped after the third ring. "Of course, cell service is spotty."

They'd exited a busy highway onto a long winding road with one lane going each direction. Dense trees stood on one side of the road. The other side had a steep embankment that dropped off into God knew what horror-filled forest.

"All right, let's not panic," she said, studying her own phone.

"I'm not panicking. I'm frustrated that we're going to be behind schedule." He raked his hair with his hands.

"Your precious schedule is the least of our problems. I don't have a strong signal either, but I think we should continue calling for help and flag down any vehicles that pass by."

A car hadn't passed them on the road since they'd stopped, but Jolene made a reasonable suggestion. They didn't have many options.

"What are you doing?" she asked as he strode closer to the fuming truck.

"I grew up around mechanics. It can't hurt to tinker around and see if we can fix it."

"Okay, while you try to MacGyver the truck, I'll walk along the road and see if I can get a better signal."

"Don't get eaten by a bear."

"Don't worry about me, *you* should make sure you don't get electrocuted. I won't try to resuscitate. I'll just roll you down the mountain," she said as she walked off.

"Hey," he called after her, "if I do get electrocuted, you won't have to pretend to be cordial."

"Why wait for death?" she asked as she threw up her middle finger at him without turning around.

He caught himself smiling.

After her calls dropped for fifteen minutes, Jolene finally got through. The AAA representative on the line assured her that a *real* mechanic and a transport vehicle would be on its way. The news made the fact that she hadn't seen a single car less worrisome.

It also allowed her to indulge in the fantasy of air conditioning. Under the sun's angry rays, that damn natural process of sweating kicked in, and Jolene could feel sweat accumulating on her neck and on her back. She even suspected that an organ or two currently malfunctioned. But help was on its way, and if she could sit in the van as she waited, she could curb the frustration that burned to be expressed in some sort of tantrum.

Hopefully, Jason would stay outside. It was baffling how one moment they could be having a genuine conversation about family and the next hurling insults at one another. It wasn't Jolene's character. She couldn't let him get under her skin like that. As she drew closer to the van, Jason emerged from under the hood of the vehicle, with the front of his T-shirt marred with black oil.

"Did you get through?" he asked, wiping his stained palms on his already dirty T-shirt.

"They said they'd be here in one to two hours."

"I guess we just hang out in the truck and try not to die in this heat." He used the back of his hand to wipe the sweat from his brow but left a mark across his forehead.

"You've got some—" Jolene gestured toward her own face.

Jason moved to the outside mirror on the passenger side of the truck to assess the damage. He mumbled a few words to himself, and then without warning, he took his shirt off. Jolene's lips parted involuntarily.

Her breath came out in tiny silent bursts. It wasn't like she'd never seen a bare-chested man before. She had probably seen thousands. Hello, spring break 2007, anyone? But the memory of gross twenty-something dudes who used their student loan money to hang loose in Puerto Vallarta and whose diets consisted of steroids and beer somehow didn't compare to the experience of seeing Jason's chiseled, bronze torso.

She got her view of his ornate and detailed tattoo on his massive left shoulder and upper arm. The hard lines his muscular body created had her slipping into musings of what it would feel like to rub her breasts against the solid surface of his chest. Those great ridges of his abs would harden her nipples and would be the source of her damnation.

Like discovering water in a desert was a mirage, a clean T-shirt appeared and interrupted Jolene's view of him. She raised her gaze and caught Jason's smug expression. Her face warmed.

"I guess you get to see my tattoo after all."

And Jolene could swear he flexed his biceps. She would not let him think it impressed her, but she didn't trust herself to say anything at the moment lest her voice betray her.

Damn him.

Chapter 4

THEY'D BEEN SITTING in the confines of the truck's cab for close to an hour. A few vehicles had passed them by, but they'd let them go without hailing for them because they still expected help to arrive. Jolene, perhaps because of some need to be productive, removed her work from her suitcase. But she soon abandoned it to lie against the seat like a carcass. Jason read a medical trade magazine, but he flipped through the issue without absorbing any of the content. Even if they'd wanted to talk, the heat left them needing to conserve energy.

Only after another two hours had passed and the sun, a constant antagonist, abated did Jason accept that they needed to think of Plan B. It wouldn't be a stretch to assume the mechanic and transport vehicle wouldn't make it before the sun set in an hour. He wished they'd taken the route that Nicole and Ty chose. But at the time, it seemed acceptable to take the shorter more rural route because they'd be driving through it during the day, whereas Ty and Nicole needed the better lit urban highways as they drove several hours behind them at night.

"We should call a cab," she said.

But it turned out that being beyond city limits meant Ubers were unavailable, and cab drivers didn't jump at the opportunity to pick them up. Once it got dark, the few drivers that did pass them refused to stop. Jason couldn't blame them. They looked extremely sketchy. But Jolene, on a mission to get someone to stop, practically stood in the middle of the road with her hip cocked and peered down the empty road.

Jason had to clench his jaw and stuff his hands in his pockets to quell his reaction. The woman wanted to get run over, but Jason knew mentioning the danger of standing in the middle of the road would make Jolene stay in that position just to spite him. So, he simply prepared himself to tackle her out of the way if a car appeared from nowhere and decided brakes didn't need employment.

"Oh. Oh! Someone's coming," Jolene said, frantically waving her arms in the air at the approaching vehicle.

A minivan driven by a middle-aged woman stopped. She only cracked her window open a little bit, but she sounded sympathetic to the plight that Jolene described, and she said, "That really sucks."

Soccer equipment for her daughter's tournament filled the interior of the car. She apologized about her inability to give them a ride but offered to pray for them.

"We're really living the beginning of a true crime TV movie," Jolene said.

She abandoned her post in the middle of the road and joined him against the side of the van. The pleasant, daytime sounds slowly gave way to noises that consisted of crickets and distant howling of some type of canine.

"Listen, I was being a dick earlier. The truck could've broken down even if I were the one driving."

She turned her entire body toward him. "I'm glad you realize that you're a judgmental person."

He spun to face her. "I'm not judgmental."

She scrunched her face and held up her thumb and pointer finger a distance apart. "Just a bit."

He frowned. "I make assessments and usually have solid opinions." His frown deepened as a smile grew on her face.

"I can admit when I'm wrong," he insisted.

"I know. I just complimented you on it."

He let out an extended breath. "It's been a long day. I don't have the energy to fight with you."

"Who said we were fighting? This is simply an analysis of your character flaws."

"Character—" He looked at her. "No, we're not doing this." He turned away from her to emphasize his resolve.

Jason could feel her readying to say something else, but before that could happen, a small powder-blue truck with rusting sides made its way down the road, stopping and honking once it was near. They both clambered toward the vehicle, desperate for some sort of lifeline.

"You folks need some help?" A man with a baseball cap and an entirely denim outfit asked from the driver's seat.

"Yes, our moving van broke down, and the towing company has been a no-show," Jason said.

The man in the truck gave both him and Jolene an assessing look up and down after listening to their story. Jason assumed the moving van lent them some credibility.

"All right, I can give you a lift." He pulled off to the side of the road just in front of the van.

The two of them gathered their personal belongings and secured the vehicle, and Jason found himself sitting in the man's cramped truck next to Jolene. It wouldn't be such a big deal if her thigh weren't pressed against his. He tried to create distance, but there was only so much space he could make before he was in the other man's lap. When his attempts failed, Jason resigned himself to the feel of Jolene's soft thigh pressed up next to his. He was aware of her like he never previously was. It troubled him for many reasons. He wouldn't deny the thrill that invaded him when he caught Jolene staring at his naked torso, but he chalked the feeling up to shock. Why should he care that she found him attractive?

"My name's Terry, by the way."

"Jolene."

"Jason." He gave Terry a handshake. "Thank you for helping us out."

"Don't mention it. I'm taking you to the closest town, Gregory Lake. It's small, not much to it really, but you'll find a place to sleep for the night."

"We really appreciate it," Jolene said. "We were worried there for a moment that we might have to sleep in the van."

"No, that wouldn't have been good. It can get pretty cold up here at night."

Before long, Jolene and Terry chatted like they were old buddies. Jason attempted to engage, but their conversation fell into the background once Jolene leaned over Jason to get a clear view of Terry as they spoke. Her mango-coconut scent still clung to her hair, and Jason wanted nothing more than to bury his face in her curls. It also didn't help that when the truck hit a bump, Jolene stabilized herself with his upper thigh. He looked down, half expecting to see seared flesh and denim where her hand had been.

They'd just concluded a thorough discussion of a cover

artist Jason had never heard of when Terry asked, "How long have you folks been an item?"

Jason's response came out rushed and urgent. "Oh, we're not a couple. Just—"

"Friends," Jolene offered.

Terry gave them a nod and a look that Jason couldn't interpret.

In an attempt to regain something he'd lost a grip on, Jason said, "Trust me, Terry, we're barely even that."

Jolene gave him a small jab in his side with her elbow and drew her mouth into a straight line.

Perhaps sensing the tension, Terry pulled down his visor to reveal a photograph of a woman in her fifties with white-blond hair and a large smile. His voice took on a sappy quality when he said, "Me and my lady, Eileen, have been together twenty-three years."

"That's amazing. Congrats," Jason said. He supposed it would be nice to have that sort of relationship. Terry was obviously happy. His mom had been happy with his father too. But getting to that point required dating, and at this time, that seemed exhaustingly tedious.

"Wow, I love that. You'll have to tell me the secret. I was literally married for three months," Jolene said.

Jason's head almost left his shoulders from the way he turned it to look at Jolene after her admission. She didn't meet his eyes. He'd forgotten that she'd been married. He tried to rack his brain for details Ty had told him over the years about Jolene, but nothing came up. Why did she get a divorce? Did she still talk to her ex-husband? The questions rolled into one solid ball of curiosity, but he knew he had no right to any of the answers, so he clenched his jaw and tried to focus on the conversation that went on without him.

"I can't really say I have a secret. I just try to make her

happy, and she does the same. And once you get on the same page about the big things like kids and money," Terry continued, "then you can have fun learning the silly things about the other person like their favorite meal. Eileen's is chicken parmesan." Terry looked away from the road for a moment at Jolene. "Did he cheat on you or something?"

Jolene laughed. Jason strained his ear to detect a hint of bitterness or sadness.

"Nothing like that. Toby is a great guy. We just got married way too young, too fast, and our lives took us in different directions."

Terry made a sympathetic *tsk*ing sound.

"I'm sorry," Jason said. And he did mean it.

Jolene shrugged, turning her face up to his. "It's okay. I'm not torn up about it anymore. The last I heard, he and his girlfriend had a child on the way. He's happy. I'm happy."

Though it was dark outside, and he could barely make out her features, he desperately wanted to confirm that she was indeed happy.

An hour later and armed with enough information to write Terry's biography, the trio arrived in the small town of Gregory Lake.

"It's more touristy than anything. There're all sorts of retreats that happen here year round. And there's a few cafes and a great pub too," Terry said.

The streetlights illuminated quiet sidewalks with charming flower baskets at every corner. They pulled into the motel's parking lot, and Jason hoped that the car-filled lot didn't mean there were no rooms available.

"Don't forget to look up Eileen's Etsy store," Terry

shouted through his open window as both Jason and Jolene thanked and wished him well.

The checking-in process was easy enough, but as the full parking lot had indicated, the motel had a lot of guests and not many rooms remained.

"This is it," Jason said as they entered their room.

Of course, there was only one bed. Why should anything go right today? The bed took up most of the space, and a smell emanated from the surfaces in the room. It was a mix of mildew and an off-brand pine-scented air freshener. Jason dumped his backpack and Jolene's suitcase in front of two chairs near the door.

"I promise not to touch you...unless you want me to," Jolene said with a smirk. "But that might piss your girl-friend off." She went to sit on the edge of the bed and almost missed. She hoisted one leg in the air to remove one shoe, then the other.

He liked the idea of her touching him, but he dashed the image out of his mind as quickly as it had come. "I don't have a girlfriend."

His comment didn't seem to register to Jolene; she looked utterly exhausted. She'd fallen asleep for the last bit of the trip, and now her lids hung half-open and her body swayed a bit.

"You can use the bathroom first," he said.

"No, no, you go first. I'm going to rest for a second."

She lay on her back with her arm slung across her eyes. He wondered how much of her fatigue had to do with their long day and how much resulted because she wasn't a night owl. Since he'd spent years and years even before dental school doing all-nighters and running on fumes, it fascinated him to see someone so easily defeated before midnight.

After fishing his toiletries from his backpack, Jason quickly brushed and flossed his teeth and took the quickest of showers. He entered the room and found Jolene completely knocked out above the covers. Deciding against waking her, he turned off the lights and slid onto the bed, not bothering to get under the covers either. The bed groaned under his weight, and he settled into a position as far away from Jolene's body as possible, turning his back toward her. Jolene's soft breathing was the last thing he consciously registered before he succumbed to sleep.

Chapter 5

MUTED and unfamiliar noises woke Jolene. It took her a few moments to remember where she was. The discolored blinds on the window helped. Disoriented and slow, she tried to move, but her body was unnaturally heavy. She quickly concluded that limbs weighed her down. Jason's forearm draped around her middle and his large hand cupped her breast. One massive leg was pinned between her legs, and her back pressed up against what could only be described as a mountain of chest.

The memories of her talking way too much on their journey to Gregory Lake flooded back. And it was the memory of the discussion about her ex-husband that made her want to bury her face in the pillow. She was no longer ashamed she'd gotten divorced after only three months of marriage, but ever since she'd inelegantly revealed the information to her sister's wedding guests, she'd tried to harp on it less. How was she to move forward if she always reminded other people of her past failures?

By the time they'd arrived at their destination, she'd

talked herself into exhaustion. She fell onto the bed without even assessing her surroundings. She could've entered the bed with the actual Devil himself, and she wouldn't have cared. But this was no devil. Her body came alive with the awareness of Jason's body, and she could feel a slow thrum of desire start in her lower stomach and end in her clit. She was certain this wasn't the position they'd fallen asleep in.

For a few minutes she contemplated the best way to disentangle herself from Jason's embrace. She fought the desire to be lulled back to sleep by his shallow breathing, and she shifted to see if she could wiggle free without waking him up. Having them both aware of how they spent the night together would cause unnecessary awkwardness. But once she moved her body, she was met with an erection that pressed against her jean-clad butt. She stifled a moan and resisted the urge to rub against it.

This is ridiculous.

With a focus that came from sporadically attending yoga classes and agility that lingered years after she stopped sneaking out of her adolescent bedroom window, Jolene got out of the bed. She slowly removed the hand that cupped her breast and shifted off the bed like a slinky moving down the stairs. Unfortunately, the action, though aptly executed, happened too fast, and she couldn't brace herself before she banged her head against the lampshade on the side table. The impact sent her reeling backwards onto the floor. Her palms stung as they made contact with the carpet. The commotion and the alarmed yelp she let out woke Jason. He stood, immediately on alert. He saw her slumped on the questionably clean motel carpet, and the next thing she knew he hauled her up and placed her on the edge of the bed as he knelt before her.

"I'm fine," she said as she gingerly touched the sore spot on her head.

He studied her for a moment, running his intense eyes up her form. The walls closed in.

"Did I push you off the bed?" he asked with a voice husky and deep from sleep. A faint crease formed between his brows as he frowned.

The sound of his voice had her clenching the bedcovers on either side of her. "Do you usually push people you sleep with off the bed?"

A small smile appeared. "No, but I don't usually fall asleep with acquaintances in my bed."

She tilted her head. He had to have a lot of people propositioning him. He was good-looking.

More than good-looking: sexy, rugged—

Did that mean he didn't do casual sex, or that he typically left immediately after casual hookups?

"You should take your jeans off and soak them before they stain," he said, pointing to where her rug-burned hands had transferred a trivial amount of blood onto her jeans.

She snorted. "Does that work on your girlfriend?"

"You keep bringing up this imaginary girlfriend of mine. I don't know where you're getting your information from." He swept an errant curl from her face, lingering for a second on where she hit her head.

Her brain short-circuited.

Deep breaths.

"Wait. When did I bring up your girlfriend?"

"One, there's no 'girlfriend,'" he said, putting air quotes around the word. "And last night you told me you wouldn't touch me and upset my girlfriend."

Of course her lethargic self would betray her like this. Her tired self might be a bit more poised than her drunken self but not by any noteworthy degree. "I actually don't care about your relationship status."

His smile grew.

"And you can stop hovering. I won't slip into a coma or anything," she said.

He let out a short laugh, then, and the deep, burly frequency turned her already humming body on fire. She then became aware of how gross she must look. She caught a whiff of cheap motel soap on his skin. He must've showered last night, and God that meant he'd rubbed up against her as she slept in day-old clothes and while she smelled like sweat and dirt. What if she had dried-up drool on her face or that gross crust stuff in the corner of her eyes?

The urgency to get away from him intensified, and she heard the angels start to sing when Jason said, "Why don't you use the washroom, and I'll call the front desk about what we can do for breakfast. Then we can figure out this mess we're in."

———

They sat in a restaurant a short walk away from their motel room. The Sunday morning patrons of the Hive Diner easily filled the large restaurant that had well-worn booths, pastel-colored walls, and a staff that smiled only when they thought someone was watching.

"I hope the repairs don't cost too much," Jason said as they settled into their booth.

"We'll split the cost, and you'll just have to remember to get the invoice so Ty and Nicky can pay you back."

He practically balked at her comment. "I'm not letting Ty and Nicole pay these extra expenses."

Jolene blinked.

"They set us off in a perfectly good vehicle, and they already have to deal with other moving costs. Besides they're my friends," he said.

"You've been paying for gas this entire time, and I let you because I assumed you were going to get your money back."

He shrugged.

"No. I'll have to pay you back for the money you've spent so far."

"It's fine."

"You're not obligated. We're not friends."

He looked at her over the brim of his mug. His eyes appeared more like brown topaz the way the light from the window hit his face.

No, brown eyes. He has ordinary brown eyes.

"Then just count it as something nice I'm doing for an acquaintance."

"If you're so eager to throw your money away, be my guest."

"I didn't grow up with much, barely anything actually. So, it's not about wanting to part with the good money I now earn."

She had the sense to know that she'd been schooled or told off somehow, and it made her slightly uncomfortable, but she held his gaze. "In that case, thank you."

His eyebrows rose like he hadn't expected sincerity from her.

"We'll split costs from here on out, though," she said.

He nodded his agreement.

Just as her stomach grew tired of waiting, Rowena—their waitress—delivered their food. She had proven to be a sullen type, communicating with as few words as possible.

"Enjoy," Rowena said over her shoulder before disappearing to help other customers.

Jolene took a couple bites of her waffles while eying the bacon that Jason had chosen as a side to his pancakes. Without much thought, Jolene reached over the table and grabbed a slice from his plate.

She froze. "God, I'm sorry." She'd only take such liberties with her sister, best friend, or her parents. Not with a virtual stranger. She blamed their sleeping arrangement for creating a false sense of intimacy. First, you feel a man's erection, then the next thing you know, you feel entitled to his literal bacon.

A faint smile appeared on his face. "Take it."

"Sorry, it's a habit. One I clearly can't turn off when I'm not in my usual company."

"We wouldn't want you to be anything but yourself, now would we?"

Embarrassment no longer goaded her.

"Oh? What's that supposed—"

"How are the first few bites?" Rowena asked. Her reappearance ended the bickering before it had a chance to start.

"Great."

"Awesome, thanks."

Rowena reached over their plates to refill their water glasses. "You folks up here for the writer's retreat?" she asked without any real curiosity and as if she read from a script.

"No, we're just passing through," Jason said.

"Our trip, unfortunately, has taken a turn. Our moving van decided to die on us," Jolene elaborated.

Rowena straightened and met their eyes. "You're getting it repaired in Gregory Lake?"

Jolene nodded. "We're getting it towed here from where it broke down an hour away. It's probably already here."

Jolene looked to Jason for confirmation, but he met her with an annoyed look.

Okay.

"You need to ask for Joey—"

The bell over the diner's door rang, and Rowena excused herself, leaving behind her cloying floral perfume.

"We shouldn't be broadcasting our business to strangers," Jason said in a hushed tone.

Jolene rolled her eyes. "Relax. I'm just making small talk."

"You never know—"

"As I was saying," Rowena reappeared as suddenly as she had left, "ask for Joey. Don't let Steve touch the truck, the man's a klutz. He'll screw up your truck more than it already is. Joey's the best, and he's married to my cousin so if you tell him I sent you, I'm sure he'll give you a good deal."

"That's fantastic, thank you," Jolene said while she gave Jason a pointed look. Manners and a smile could get you a long way.

"Yes, thank you."

"And," Rowena continued, drawing out the word with enthusiasm that didn't appear to come naturally to her, "I'll tell you what, if you guys are still here during lunchtime, there's free dessert with your names on it."

"Ah, Rowena, a woman after my own heart. Thank you," Jolene said and gave Jason another smug look.

After breakfast, they got a taxi to the auto body repair shop where their traitorous moving van waited for them. They'd been lucky that despite it being a Sunday, the shop opened for several hours. The environment brought back memories for Jason—the smell of oil and fumes and the high-pitched sounds of drills and motors.

Joey, the highly recommended mechanic, accommodated them and prattled on in a way his cousin-in-law did not. Joey used stories and metaphors to express how the moving van needed a new thermostat and a radiator flush. It sounded expensive, and Jason silently thanked Jolene for getting them a deal through her oversharing. He didn't actually thank her, however, because then he'd know no peace.

"Simon, here"—Joey gestured toward the man with floppy, blond hair who'd suddenly appeared—"will get you a drink, and you can take a seat in our waiting area."

The service time didn't take long. Two lukewarm cups of water and dull conversation with other customers later, he and Jolene stood with their newly repaired moving van in an open area just outside the shop. They waited for the front desk clerk, Simon, to bring them their receipt and keys. Jolene fanned herself with a brochure she'd picked up and aimlessly walked around the truck.

"I never thought I'd be wishing for West Coast rain," she groaned. "I'm not built for this heat."

Jason would beg to differ. She wore this bright orange, cotton dress that looked great against her dark skin, and it hugged her breasts and waist before billowing out to a skirt that stopped just above her knees. She looked sweet and tantalizing, like an orange Creamsicle in the dead of summer.

"I swear I haven't stopped sweating since we started this trip," she said, disappearing from view once again as she made her third turn around the truck.

He busied himself looking through Google Maps for

nearby gas stations. It would probably be best to fill up before they got back to the motel. That way they could just head out and finish this obviously damned trip. He got caught up in modifying their itinerary until the sound of Jolene's scream yanked him to the present and sent his heartbeat into a frenzied rhythm.

Chapter 6

JOLENE BAXTER, at the age of twenty-seven, didn't think about death often. Today, however, her mortality decided to introduce itself.

She had noticed the heavy-duty latch that secured the back door on the moving van was disengaged. Confused, Jolene had tugged the sliding door and confirmed that it was indeed unlocked. She hoisted the door to peer inside the back of the van, but unfortunately for her, death waited in the form of a beady-eyed, fast-moving raccoon.

The raccoon had been prepared for an invasion because once Jolene slid the door high enough, the beast propelled its body toward her face. To Jolene's utter amazement and relief, she ducked out of the raccoon's reach. And the animal made a choice not to continue to fight but rather parkour into the distance.

"Jolene. What's wrong?" Jason stood in front of her, grasping her upper arms painfully, his face a sheet of worry and dread.

Her heart still pounded. "A fucking raccoon just jumped out of the back of the van," she screeched.

"What?" He still grasped her arms.

"A gross-looking, mangy raccoon just tried to claw my eyes out."

"Are you hurt?" He scanned her face, neck, and body.

"No, I'm fine. It didn't touch me."

"How the hell did a raccoon get into the back of the van?" he asked as they both turned to look into said van.

A moment of stunned silence ran between them.

"Holy shit."

The truck wasn't empty. No, it would have been too kind to immediately realize that they'd been robbed. Instead, Jolene stood there trying to decipher if she'd imagined more things in the truck. But key pieces she'd distinctly remembered seeing had disappeared, like the microwave and a pair of lamps.

"They took the rug." She laughed.

They looked at each other, trying to silently confirm that they indeed saw what the other saw.

"I—" Jason said.

"What—"

They stood there for several minutes, letting the gravity of their situation settle into place in their minds.

"You folks are good to go now," Simon, the front desk clerk for the shop called out as he walked toward them. He rounded the corner of the van dangling its keys. "Is everything okay?"

Jolene and Jason both turned to the man with matching dazed looks. Poor Simon shifted nervously under Jason and Jolene's bewildered gazes before seemingly deciding whatever the problem, it wasn't his fault and he'd fulfilled his job description. He placed the keys on the edge of the truck's steps and gave a strained smile and backed away until he disappeared inside the building.

"What are we going to do?" Jolene finally asked.

The question went unanswered for a while. And it might have remained that way if Jason wasn't Jason.

He counted off each point with his fingers. "Okay. We're going to contact the authorities, book another day in our room, and see Rowena about those free desserts."

The police station in Gregory Lake was surprisingly robust. A constable had asked questions, taken a statement, and promised to be in touch very soon. The process hadn't provided any solutions other than waiting. And Jolene debated whether or not to fill in her sister on how the cute little Hallmark Christmas movie town they'd just stopped in to repair the moving van had become the backdrop of an investigation that would take an indiscernible amount of time. The only thing that had gone right was that they'd managed to rebook their flights for early Tuesday morning.

Jolene could practically hear the wheels in Jason's head spin as they, along with their free cinnamon buns from the Hive Diner, made their way from the motel's front desk back to their room. They'd been forced to rebook their one-bed motel room.

"We'll have to call Ty and Nicole," Jolene said almost to herself. Her sister would've already arrived.

"We should see what the police find before unnecessarily stressing them out. I think being honest about—"

Jason probably said something reasonable that she'd ultimately agree with, but his voice faded into the background, melding in with the noise from the street. Something in the back of an SUV parked four doors down from their room caught Jolene's eye.

"Jolene?" Jason followed her line of sight. "What are you looking at?"

"I think I see my sister's bike helmet," she said in a hushed tone. She made a detour toward the vehicle. Her gaze trained on a silver helmet pressed up against the right back door window.

"Jolene, wait."

She didn't listen, and by the time she'd arrived at the car, she'd convinced herself that her sister's helmet sat inside. "This is hers." She punctuated her statement with pokes toward the helmet.

Jason looked between her and the helmet. "Are you sure?"

"One hundred percent."

His eyebrows shot up.

"Okay, maybe seventy-five percent."

Jason let out a long breath.

"It's in the car; they're obviously trying to hide it." She pointed toward two bicycles chained to the posts in front of a motel door. "They have their bicycles out but kept the helmets in."

"You know that's weak logic."

"They probably have more of our stuff in here," Jolene mumbled. She circled the car, leaning close and peering through the tinted windows.

Jason's hands settled on her shoulders, not moving her but simply suggesting she back away a bit.

"Jolene, let's just think about this for a second. We can call the constable we spoke with, and she can come and do her job."

Still absorbed with her bootleg Nancy Drew investigation, Jolene ignored him. They shouldn't have left the van unattended all night. If the authorities couldn't find Nicole and Ty's things, it would be another headache the couple had to contend with. Jolene wanted to test the doors on the driver's side of the car. Where this boldness came from, she would have to dissect later.

Jason groaned. And perhaps sensing her irrationality, he finally grabbed her waist and tugged her away from the car. "Jolene."

"Don't use that tone with me. This is our fault. We need to fix it."

"We literally just got back from—"

"Can we help you?" a voice behind them asked.

Jolene and Jason both whirled around. A slim, very tall man and a similarly slim and equally as tall woman stood before them. Everything about them looked sharp. They had angular features, the woman's hair fell in blunt sheets against her shoulders, and they both wore all black athletic wear. Jolene decided that they looked like really attractive James Bond villains.

"We are so sorry—"

"It's not what it looks like—" Jason and Jolene said simultaneously.

The pair's brows furrowed as they studied Jolene and Jason. The woman looked as if she was a second away from calling the police on them. Jolene forced herself to run through a Rolodex of plausible excuses because the truth didn't seem like an adequate reason to creep around a car like she'd been doing.

"We're staying right over there"—Jolene gestured in the general direction of their room—"and we're in the market for a new vehicle and your car caught our eye. It's embarrassing how carried away I get—like I'm at a car dealership or tradeshow," Jolene said with all the sweetness and ditziness she could imbue in her voice.

The suspicion and uncertainty remained stark in the tall couple's eyes.

"Yes. She forgets it's not normal to prowl around strangers' cars," Jason said.

Jolene's smile faltered a fraction but sheer grit and literal fear that they would get in actual trouble kept it plastered in place.

One moment the strangers' faces projected apprehension, and the next moment the man's face split with a smile. "She's the same way when we go to open houses. Touching counters, cabinets, floors."

The men laughed like they'd just both highlighted something quite novel about women. To Jason's credit, his laugh sounded a little off, nowhere near natural. The tall woman playfully pinched the man, cutting his laugh short. He gave her a quick peck on her cheek and rubbed the area she had pinched.

"They make fun of us, but they don't realize it's our attention to detail that prevents them from making bad spending decisions," the woman said.

Jolene nodded, and it dawned on her that she and Jason had somehow stumbled their way out of their current predicament, but in the process, the couple in front of them had concluded that they, too, were a couple.

"I'm Megan. And this is my husband, Cliff."

"Jolene and Jason," Jason said.

Megan and Cliff eyed them curiously, and Jolene blamed the decidedly not-so-very-couple distance between her and Jason. She shifted her body till her side touched Jason's, and Jason in turn awkwardly slung his arm over her shoulder, obviously picking up on the role they had unceremoniously been cast in. They might as well have ended their pose with a ta-da just to emphasize the strangeness of the situation. But whatever the real couple saw, melted the last worry lines that marked their perfect faces.

"It's nice to meet both of you," Megan said.

"Likewise," Jolene said.

"You should join us. We're going to the diner for a late lunch. We can tell you all about the car," Megan suggested.

"We've already eaten," Jason said, conveniently holding up the Styrofoam containers that held their cinnamon buns.

They hadn't actually eaten a proper meal yet.

"And we have somewhere to be in thirty minutes," Jolene quickly added to further secure their escape.

"That's unfortunate, maybe we can grab coffee or breakfast another time, then?" Cliff asked.

"That sounds lovely," Jolene said but made no effort to pinpoint exactly when this coffee grabbing or breakfast thing would happen.

Jason quickly extracted them from Megan and Cliff's presence, and they left with strained smiles in place.

In the privacy of their motel room, Jason turned to Jolene and was prepared to scold her for her carelessness, but Jolene burst into a fit of giggles. Her face lit up, and she threw her head back, causing her curls to move about. The sight caught Jason off guard. Had he ever seen her this... elated? It stopped any harsh remarks he had for her. Jolene's laughter died when she noticed he wasn't similarly amused.

"Don't tell me you're actually mad," she said.

It would be nice if he had an emotion like anger to cling onto because his growing awareness of her troubled and complicated things. This trip should have been drawing to a close with nothing changed between them. But now Jason noticed how the place she'd hit her head this morning looked a bit bruised, and he wanted to run his lips lightly over it. And speaking of lips, Jolene's pouty lips had a slight sheen from the tinted lip balm she reapplied periodically. Those lips hailed to him now, and before he could think of the dozen reasons it would be a bad idea, he kissed her.

One moment Jolene mentally prepared for Jason's reprimand, and in the next Jason's lips pressed against hers. She immediately melted against him like she'd been hoping, waiting for this. His firm body enveloped her, and she'd never felt so dainty. Every point of her body that made contact with his buzzed, and her body woke up from a slumber it hadn't been aware it took. She had enough experience that a mere kiss shouldn't have shaken her, but nevertheless, if his hands hadn't bracketed her waist, Jolene might've floated away into sheer bliss.

His lips caressed hers, and their lips parted. Warmth emanated from him, and he tasted faintly like lemon. His tongue traced the shape of her lips before searching, exploring further. She let her tongue roam, and the heat that rushed through her when their tongues met had her gripping his biceps. They each took and gave. And when Jolene gently caught his bottom lip between her teeth and worried it for a moment, the groan that escaped from him became her own. The sound travelled through her and began a steady ache in her lower abdomen. She pressed her body closer to his, feeling her nipples harden. She lost herself in the sensation. But as abruptly as the kiss had started, similarly it ended. Jason ripped himself away from her, and Jolene practically whimpered at the loss of contact.

Through their labored breathing, Jason stared at her, and the desire she saw in his eyes tempted her to drop her panties and beg. But *that* would be worse than her decision to respond to his kiss. But they couldn't just stay there staring at each other and breathing as if they were trying to fog up a mirror.

In an attempt to reset and possibly slow down her heart rate, Jolene shrugged. "That was okay."

Jason gave her still-hard nipples a look, and it seemed like he might go in for another kiss just to underscore her lie. But his jaw tightened and without touching her or saying anything else, he left the motel room.

Chapter 7

THE PUB WAS loud and hectic, but it served Jolene well because her stomach rumbled. She'd eaten her cinnamon bun then had taken a nap. Blessedly, she hadn't dreamed about Jason. She might've tossed and turned for a while, but the important thing was she eventually slept. He'd returned to their room an hour later, and he'd acted like nothing had happened so she did the same.

However, the sparks that had jumped between them when they'd kissed still lingered. They moved in their small quarters in polite silence. One watched television while the other read some uninteresting thing. When Jolene had broken their silence to suggest they go to the gift shop before it closed, he'd replied as if he was giving a stranger directions. The bland and stilted atmosphere between them had Jolene believing her reaction to Jason had been a fluke, simply a side effect of going so long without a pleasant kissing experience. But then she and Jason reached for the same knickknack in the gift shop, a grizzly bear on its hind legs holding a plaque with the town's name on it. Their hands connected, and Jolene had felt as if she'd put her finger into an electrical socket.

Now, she and Jason navigated the high tables and stools in the pub. The cramped space forced them to make occasional contact, and it jarred her equilibrium every time. They found a spot at the back, near an already packed patio and close to a stage of some kind.

They didn't speak. It didn't bother her at all. Not one bit. Small talk was overrated anyway. But she couldn't help but feel disappointed at the familiar dynamic. She'd slowly begun to believe they'd moved past their tense interactions.

"It's a cool place," Jolene finally said.

He simply nodded, looking around. Their waiter appeared then, a beacon of human interaction that Jolene appreciated. Once the waiter left with their orders, the pub's noise filled the silence between them.

"I called Nicky," Jolene said.

"Oh, yeah?"

"Yeah, I didn't tell her about the theft, but I told her we're still having car problems."

"All right."

She wanted to scream. Did he not get that, if left to her own thoughts, she would concoct all sorts of scenarios in her mind that would make sleeping in the same bed tonight absolute torture? But the silence dragged on until the waiter returned with their drinks.

"Whew," Jolene said, screwing her face up at the strong rum that hit her. "The bartender has a generous hand."

"Careful, now."

She rolled her eyes.

Condescending asshole.

But it was the first thing he'd said post-kiss that sounded like his usual self and that made her relax a fraction.

This wasn't him. In the last twenty-four hours Jason felt like he waded through sand. He thrived when in control of his life, situations, and emotions. And till this point, he had a firm grip on them all. The chaotic trip, this woman, and the nagging feeling he had in his chest were disastrous developments. He tried to erect the boundaries that had somehow been compromised in the last day. Could it be just yesterday that he'd dreaded this trip because he thought Jolene would annoy him? He wished she annoyed him. And he wished he hadn't responded to her touch earlier and she hadn't fit so perfectly against him.

She acted as if nothing had happened and so did he, but it irked him that the kiss hadn't affected her as it had him. She just chatted and tried to draw conversation from him as if he didn't currently fight the image of her bent over the very bar stool she sat on, begging him to take her. He'd literally fled their motel room, and now he dreaded the eventual moment they'd be confined to their room once again.

"I'm just going to quickly wash my hands," she said as she hopped off the stool and disappeared into the ever-growing busyness of the pub.

For the first time since arriving, the tension in his shoulders relented. But it was short-lived because someone dragged their hand across his back as they moved to face him. A woman, with clear intentions, leaned toward him and almost dipped her long hair into his drink.

She practically purred. "Hey, there."

After Jolene washed her hands and confirmed a pimple

hadn't managed to sprout from nowhere, she squeezed her way past the bar's patrons back to her table. Before she arrived, she zeroed in on the woman who was chatting up Jason. The tinge of jealousy that sprung up couldn't be reasoned with. But with effort, she placed a blank expression on her face and drew closer to the table.

The woman looked appropriately dressed and dolled up for a night out. And Jolene in that moment regretted not packing anything more than an eyebrow pencil and lip balm. At the time it seemed sensible. Her ego wouldn't have allowed her to wear overly tight jeans *and* bring her entire makeup kit under the pretense it wasn't for Jason.

The woman then placed a hand on Jason's forearm, and Jolene felt the world tilt for a second. Jolene's visceral reaction to the scene playing out in front of her disturbed her, and she fortified her resolve to remain expressionless. She hoisted herself up onto her stool and willed herself to sip her drink and not stare. Jolene, however, didn't expect the woman to turn toward her, horrified.

"Is this your girlfriend?" the woman asked, taking a healthy step away from Jason.

"Oh, no, no!" Jolene said. "He's single."

The woman looked to Jason for confirmation, but his gaze remained fixed on Jolene.

"In that case——" The woman leaned in closely and whispered something in Jason's ear, and left their table shortly after.

Jolene had unintentionally drained more than half her drink while watching the interaction, and its effects made her woozy. She clasped her hands around her glass, encouraging herself not to say anything. That lasted for fifteen seconds.

"So, did she give you her number or her address?"

Jason who'd been people watching and nursing his own

drink turned his brown topaz eyes to her. "Neither. She just said she'd be right back and to wait for her."

Jolene battled weird emotions that she didn't care to parse out, so she gave him a saucy wag of her eyebrows to play off any turbulent feelings that might unintentionally be visible. Mercifully, she spotted their waiter with their meals, and she straightened her back and smiled as he approached.

"Here is your taco salad. And here is your chicken fettuccine," the waiter said, sliding their dishes into place in front of them. "Enjoy your meal."

And she did. They didn't exchange words, and all went well until in her periphery Jolene saw Cliff and Megan walking through the doors of the pub. Their tall frames poked through the mass of people who surrounded the bar. Jolene almost slammed her face into her taco salad trying to duck out of view of the couple.

Jason's lips turned slightly downward and his eyebrows furrowed. "What's wrong?"

"Don't look now, but that Cliff and Megan couple just walked in."

"Shit," Jason said as he also ducked his head.

"The pub is big enough. They probably won't even see us."

But then Jolene made eye contact with Cliff. She averted her gaze as if she hadn't recognized him and held her breath.

"Crap. They're walking this way."

"Jolene, Jason!" Megan said coming right up to their table with Cliff by her side.

The horror happened in slow motion for Jason. Megan

and Cliff arrived at their table, and the couple invited themselves to sit and order drinks. Jolene had to move closer to him so the stools Cliff and Megan brought with them could fit.

"We ate a late lunch," Megan explained. "We're just here for drinks and some light appetizers."

Megan and Cliff also wanted to talk. Jason and Jolene couldn't evade questions like they had before, and Jason resisted the temptation to just tell the couple the truth and finish his meal in peace. He didn't feel like concocting stories for the benefit of people he'd never see again.

But Jolene was already smiling and chatting with the couple, her hand waving in full effect. Jason suspected that she still tried to determine whether or not Megan and Cliff had stolen their things. He listened while Jolene fabricated a somewhat believable love story, and he found that the details that were actually true made him smile. For instance, she talked about the time they'd walked arm in arm as maid of honor and best man to their places at the front of the church. He'd tripped on the edge of the aisle runner, and Jolene had played the slightly embarrassing moment off by patting his back and winking at him.

"So, he's your brother-in-law's best friend, and you met during the wedding-planning process?" Megan asked.

"Pretty much," Jolene said.

"Cliff, isn't that's so cute?" Megan squealed, clapping her hands and looking between Jolene and him.

"So, you two are into biking, huh?" Jolene asked.

Jason inwardly groaned at Jolene's less-than-subtle transition.

"I saw your bikes chained up next to your door," she quickly added.

Jason wasn't entirely convinced that the couple were their thieves. And at this point, he believed with all the rapport Jolene had built with the couple, Cliff and Megan would understand if they told them the truth. But for some reason, Jason allowed the ruse to go on.

"Oh, we love it," Cliff said. "We do bike marathons every couple of years. But we're up here just to have fun."

"And we found some new bikes and helmets for this season," Megan said.

"Found?" Jolene squeaked.

"Yeah, we were searching for different bikes and accessories we could travel with. We found some online for a reasonable price a few months ago. The guy who sold it to us used to own a bike shop and was getting rid of inventory."

And with that explanation, they'd arrived at a dead end. Jason watched Jolene's smile dim and her shoulders slump slightly. The waiter arrived with Cliff and Megan's drinks and appetizers, and Jason took the opportunity to soothe some of Jolene's disappointment by leaning in close to her and saying, "Try to resist stealing their fries."

He received the small smile he wanted but also an unexpected squeeze from her at the spot just above his knee. The four of them finished their meals, and Cliff and Megan shared a dessert while Jolene ordered her second alcoholic drink. Jason discovered that Cliff and Megan were actually interesting people to talk with when he wasn't lying to their faces and he could be himself. He wasn't exactly talkative, but he found himself contributing to the conversation. They were well travelled and had done things one might consider cultured, but they didn't come off as snobbish when they talked about spending weeks in Whistler and competing in triathlons all around the world.

Jason was so absorbed in the conversation, he didn't notice that someone stood behind him until a strange hand ran across his shoulder. The woman from earlier, the one

Jason had forgotten even existed till now, had returned to fulfill her implied offer.

Earlier when the stranger had first approached Jason, he was about to let her know he wasn't interested when Jolene returned from the washroom. The look that had briefly passed on Jolene's face, however, threw him for a loop. She couldn't have been jealous. There was no way, but as he sat there and tried to decipher the intricacies of human facial expressions, the strange woman had whispered that she'd be right back.

"Hi, again," the random woman now said in his ear.

Cliff and Megan's eyebrows raised, and they cocked their heads to the side.

"Not interested," Jason said.

But his response was cut off when Jolene stood and removed the woman's hand from where it lay on his shoulder. She then grabbed his face and kissed him. It wasn't as thorough as the one they had shared earlier in the day, but the sparks that coursed through him were still strong enough that the thought Jolene probably kissed him to maintain their con didn't cross his mind.

The sound of Cliff and Megan's laughter finally drew Jason from the kiss. He hadn't even noticed the stranger had left without further protest.

"You can let me go now," Jolene said, her voice breaking a bit.

He looked down at where he still held Jolene about her waist. He kept his arms around her for a beat longer before releasing her. They turned back to their company with bashful smiles. For the second time that day, Jason had lost himself. It unnerved him to know kisses were at fault. He chanced a glance at Jolene who anxiously chewed the tip of her straw.

"Wow," Cliff said. "And I thought Meg was possessive."

Cliff and Megan left shortly after they'd finished their dessert. Jason dreaded going back to the motel room because that meant he'd have to sleep in the same bed as Jolene and contend with his attraction to her. Last night he'd been too tired to even register that he slept in bed next to her. But the day's events wouldn't make that the case tonight. So, when Jolene made no moves to end their night at the pub, he didn't either. Maybe they could stay out long enough so that when his head hit the pillow, he'd immediately fall asleep.

The buzz that had swirled in the bar still went strong, but the majority of the energy now stayed around the area surrounding the stage. The staff set up sound equipment and turned on the stage lights.

"Oh, they're doing karaoke!" Jolene exclaimed. She put her drink down and turned to him. Her eyes danced.

He bristled. "I don't know why you're looking at me like that."

"Karaoke is not your thing?"

"Crawling back to the motel on my hands and knees sounds more pleasurable," he said bluntly. The idea of standing up in front of people and doing something he wasn't 100 percent good at seemed like his version of hell.

She smiled. "I think I'm going to do it."

He remembered her pitchy voice from yesterday on the road. Did she know? "If you get booed off stage, I promise I'll whisk you out of here."

"I won't get booed off stage," she said, sounding offended.

Dear God, she didn't know.

"Actually, I think it will be quite the opposite," she said.

"How so?"

"I'll get a standing ovation."

He stared at her in disbelief. "Jolene, I don't know how to say this…but I've heard you sing—"

"I know I have a bad voice. I actually might be tone deaf. It doesn't matter. I'm going to get a standing ovation," she said with such conviction that Jason experienced a wave of mild pity for her.

"All right, then let's make this interesting."

She scrunched her nose. "What do you mean by interesting?"

"If you get a standing ovation—"

"How are we defining a standing ovation?"

"There are about"—he scanned the bar—"a hundred or so people in here. If twenty of them get out of their seats and clap for you, then I'll pay for all your meals tomorrow."

"And what if they don't?"

He wanted to ask for another kiss. "Then you'll have to give me one sincere compliment."

"Damn, so sensitive. You call a man old and boring one time…"

He gave her a mischievous smile in response.

"All right, deal." She extended her hand and he grasped it.

Jolene left her seat to sign up, and the first brave soul got on stage and sang a rendition of Britney Spears's "Toxic." He had sufficient energy, but he tried too hard to sound good. Another decided to do Queen's "Bohemian Rhapsody" that just ended with the whole pub singing along. Each section of the audience took a different harmony. Jason watched politely and clapped when appropriate. Meanwhile, Jolene enthusiastically swayed to the music and offered supportive whoops. He thought she might actually join the singer on stage that sang "Jolene" by Dolly Parton.

"This is my jam," she shouted over the music.

Several more people performed before Jolene's turn. For some reason his heart rate picked up like he was the one going up there. He reasoned that his reaction came from the stakes he had in her performance. Jolene threw her head back and finished the rest of her drink. She rotated her shoulders and shook her head like a fighter warming up to enter the wrestling ring. She made her way to the stage, and the bright lights illuminated her and the Creamsicle dress.

She tapped on the mic. "Hello, testing one, two—"

"We can hear you just fine, darlin'!" someone in the audience shouted.

"Great. My name's Jolene." A number of the patrons responded with a hello, while the beginning instrumentals of Donna Summer's "Last Dance" played.

The first note that escaped Jolene's mouth wasn't a note as such, but a squeak. It didn't improve from there. Her voice did not quite catch the right notes, and it grasped for a semblance of a melody. Though Jason involuntarily cringed at the off-putting notes she hit, he could not help but be impressed. Despite her awful voice, she sang each bad note with certainty and confidence. And the audience swayed and watched politely because karaoke didn't require singers of *The Voice* caliber.

When Jolene hit a particularly bad note, Jason mused how nice it would feel to actually receive a compliment from Jolene even if it were a forced one. Through the first verse, Jolene conservatively stepped side to side. She didn't look at the monitor that had the lyrics; she obviously knew the song very well. And once the chorus hit and the tempo picked up, a switch flipped and Jolene started to really dance.

She twirled across the stage. She shimmied her hips while pointing to individuals in the audience, and flipped her head side to side, animating her coily hair. She essentially made the stage her Soul Train line. She didn't let any beat go to waste. Jason stared in awe, and soon after caught himself grinning like a fool. The audience clapped, enthralled by her performance. By the time the song ended, the tipsy spectators were on their feet whooping and hollering. She graciously bowed and gave mock kisses to her new fans. As she made her way back toward their table, the bar's patrons gave her thumbs-up and high-fives. He breathed in the cheerfulness she exuded.

So damn beautiful.

She collapsed on her stool, looking bright-eyed and exhilarated, and before he could commend her or even take in how her hair fell in her face with nymph-like abandon, she leaned toward him. "Tomorrow I think I'd like lobster for at least one of my meals."

He gave her a good-natured laugh, but found it difficult to draw a full breath.

Chapter 8

IT WAS one a.m. when Jolene and Jason arrived at their motel room. The two drinks she'd ordered had lost their effect, and now all that occupied her mind was the thought of sleep. Well, not the actual act of sleeping, but rather the understanding that she would have to sleep in the same bed as Jason again. This time knowing for a fact how her body would respond.

"Umm, I'm going to use the washroom first."

"Yeah, go ahead," he said absentmindedly, already at the tiny desk in the room, no doubt planning tomorrow out.

She got herself showered, flossed, and brushed. Unfortunately for her, she had run out of clean underwear.

A laundromat, I need a laundromat. Tomorrow.

She also hadn't expected to share a bed with Jason on this trip, so the oversized T-shirt she packed as her version of sleepwear barely hit her upper thigh and did nothing remotely flattering. She decided to keep her bra on and slip it off when she crawled into bed while he used the bathroom. She didn't need to come out boobs jiggling.

She strategically placed her day's clothes and toiletry bag in front of her, and bent her knees so the hem of the shirt would fall as low as possible. When she left the bathroom, Jason sat on the far side of the room, reading his trade medical magazine while the news played on a low volume. He looked so...disarmingly handsome. He'd removed his shoes and slouched in the chair with his legs crossed at the ankles. An image of him in that exact pose in her own apartment sprung into her mind, and she quickly filed it in a mental drawer called "Things That Will Destroy You."

"All done?" he asked without taking his eyes away from what he read.

She made some sound in affirmation. He finally looked up, and his eyes widened slightly and perhaps they even darkened when he dragged his gaze up her body. She should have wrapped a towel around her waist.

Too late now.

He collected his things and walked to the bathroom without comment. She sprang into action the moment the bathroom door closed behind him. She quickly shuffled to her suitcase and shoved her clothes and toiletries inside. Without removing her T-shirt, she took off her bra and threw it into the bag as well. Then, as if she hadn't been rejected from her elementary school gymnastics team, she leaped into the bed and hauled the covers to her chin.

After she let the pounding of her heart settle, she debated if she should turn off some of the lights. But what if Jason tripped and hurt himself? Okay, so she would leave the lights on, but she should turn off the TV. She looked at the door. She could hear the shower running. Where was the remote? She scanned the room and found it balancing on the armrest of the chair Jason had sat on. She gave the closed bathroom door one last look before she retrieved the remote and turned the television off. Getting back into the bed, she closed her eyes and tried to relax. If she were lucky, she would fall asleep before he left the bathroom.

Relaxing things. Think about relaxing things.

She mentally conjured up her vision board, and when that didn't work, she mentally put together an outfit she'd wear to work in the upcoming week. But that didn't work either.

She opened her eyes again. Where had she put her phone?

Just leave it, Jolene.

But the nagging need to locate her phone grew. Somewhere a think piece about Millennials and technology mocked her. How long had it been? She couldn't hear the shower anymore. But he probably still brushed his teeth, and as a dentist, he definitely would floss so she had time, maybe a minute or two. She looked around the room, examining where she could have placed it. She hadn't left it at the pub. Did she take it to the bathroom?

No.

She remembered throwing it on top of her suitcase before heading to the bathroom. She must have flung it aside when she opened it the second time to return her belongings. It had to be lying somewhere on the floor. She left the safe confines of the bed once again, got on her hands and knees, and immediately spotted it under the chair. But as luck would have it, as she reached for her cell phone, the bathroom door swung open.

The cold shower and quiet jerking off worked somewhat to diffuse the lust that had rushed through Jason when he'd seen Jolene exit the bathroom. The T-shirt she wore had barely concealed her shapely legs. But all his efforts went out the window when he reentered the bedroom to see Jolene crouched down on the floor. Her gorgeous ass was visible underneath the T-shirt, and God help him, she wasn't wearing any underwear.

She clumsily got up when the door opened. And her breasts gently bounced, drawing his attention to them.

His mouth went dry.

He wanted to rush toward her and feel her body unhampered by underwear and thick fabrics, but instead, with control that would make some deity proud, he walked toward his bag to deposit his stuff. His movement kick-started Jolene's, and she scampered to the bed like the floor was lava. If he wasn't battling a hard-on, he might have been amused. When he turned around, he knew she'd been watching him because her eyes shut a little too late. She'd hoisted the sheet all the way up to her chin. He took measured breaths, turned off the lights in their room, and gingerly entered the bed. He positioned himself so his back faced her.

His thoughts moved in all sorts of directions. It would first settle or get comfortable with a safe subject or idea but quickly bounce to more dangerous visuals. The epic game of pinball his mind played made falling asleep very difficult.

"I've set my alarm for six a.m.," he said into the darkness.

"Okay," she replied in a shrill voice.

He didn't know how much time had passed before incessant ringing started. Thinking it might have come from the neighboring motel room, he didn't say anything. But it persisted.

"Is that yours?" he asked.

"Yes."

A beat passed with the ringing continuing to fill the silence.

"Are you going to answer it or at least turn it off?"

"It's under the chair."

"Okay."

"I'll need to turn on the light to get to it. You'll have to stay turned away. My top is short, and I don't have any more clean underwear."

"I know."

He sensed her turn to face him, and he willed himself not to do the same. In the dark room he wouldn't be able to make anything out, but it would be one step too close for him. It would end in him doing something ill advised.

"God, you saw my butt, didn't you?"

He didn't respond.

She groaned. "Okay, so to prevent that from happening again, just don't turn around."

The sheets rustled and the bed lightly bounced as she got out of the bed, and the lights came on a moment later. The ringing stopped, but then she said, "Shit."

"Is that a I-have-a-charley-horse-and-require-assistance shit or a more mundane this-has-been-one-long-day shit?"

"Neither."

The way she said it, without any real humor in her voice made him pause. "Jolene, can I turn now?"

"Fuck."

"Okay, I'm going to turn around…make yourself decent."

He found her slumped in the chair he had been sitting in earlier, staring intently at her phone. She worried her bottom lip.

"What's wrong?" And because he'd learned to brace himself for the worst, he added, "Is someone hurt?"

The latter question got Jolene's attention. She looked up, and he swore the tension in her face reduced a bit.

"Oh, no. Nothing like that. It's just"—she took a breath—"apparently one of the owners of the apothecary line we're launching was filmed being an asshole to a waitress, and the video has gone somewhat viral."

"Is it really bad?"

"I can't load the video, the damn WiFi sucks, but from what my team is describing, it's really, really bad."

He resisted the urge to do what came naturally to him, solving problems. "What are the implications?"

"Well, nobody wants to buy anything from assholes. Plus, our whole campaign is leaning into their brand of positivity and lightness—" Her cell rang, interrupting her explanation.

"Hey, Yvonne. No, go ahead."

Jason watched as she went into a conversation, parsing out logistics and coming up with a plan as she spoke to Yvonne on the other line. Realizing this might take a while, Jason turned the TV on and muted it before switching on the subtitles. Jolene sent him an apologetic look. He found a program on the History Channel that explored the fascinating habits of sixteenth century royalty, but he couldn't give a damn because he was focused on what Jolene did.

She sounded confident and amazingly calm seeing that failure could derail her project. So caught up in the conversation she had, Jolene paced around the room. Her breasts, freed from the constraints of a bra, moved tantalizingly. Every now and again, she would mindlessly raise her hand to her face and her T-shirt would inch up, not enough to see anything, but enough for Jason's heart to beat at a funky rhythm. He thought about how she would feel on top of him, underneath him, curled up beside him, and by the time she'd finished her call, he had a full-blown erection he tried to hide with a pillow.

"Okay, I think we've diverted an utter disaster. I'll have to send a few emails tomorrow and actually watch the video, but I'm feeling less panicked about the situation." She turned from her position across the room to face him.

And within a few seconds she must have remembered her state of undress. Maybe his intense look jogged her awareness. "God, of course I'd be flashing my nipples." She clutched her arms around herself, but that made the hem of the T-shirt rise higher than it had before.

He groaned inwardly. "Don't talk about your nipples, Jolene." His voice sounded gruff even to his own ears.

He saw the spark in her eye. Tonight, she wanted to play with fire. Obviously temporarily averting her work crisis had inspired her feisty side, and he could bet it was dangerous when added to her usual defiant character.

"Why not?" she asked as she let a small smile form.

"I'm barely hanging on here." He shocked himself and her with his honesty.

"Wh-what if I want you to let go?" she whispered.

She didn't know if he'd answer. What was she doing? She smothered the urge to say something funny to diffuse the tension and get back to sleeping. But in the face of clear evidence of his attraction to her—the way he looked at her and the bulge he did a poor job of hiding—all the reasons she fought her own attraction to Jason seemed ridiculous. So what if they weren't each other's favorite people? They were two adults who were physically attracted to each other. Surely they could act on those feelings without needing to complicate anything else.

"We don't even like each other," he said.

A counterpoint that, at best, sounded dubious when said out loud. He obviously thought the same thing because he got up from his place on the bed. His gaze trained on her lips.

"What does that matter? We won't see each other often after this trip." She drew closer to him through movement she didn't consciously make. Her hands were itching to touch his shoulders and feel the muscles underneath his shirt again. "We can go back to how things were," she said.

He smiled. "Well, I'd hope it would be a little more cordial."

Abruptly, as if finally making up his mind, he made a detour toward the desk and grabbed his phone. He plucked away at it. Jolene squirmed in the silence, trying not to stare at the way his dick pressed against his pajama bottoms. Eventually he looked up from his phone. The intensity of the moment had not abated.

He placed the shining mobile device in front of her face. "My current STI test results."

She studied the report, and everything was in order. She quickly pulled up hers, fumbling with the login information as the WiFi made things take longer than she appreciated. With each passing moment, however, she could feel the imaginary dial on her anticipation tick higher. She similarly placed her phone in front of him. He gave her a nod when he finished reading.

The desire between them moved in uninterrupted waves. Pulsing and flowing in a way that made her feel lightheaded. And just as she got ready to do something to alleviate the buildup and ease the palpable tension, Jason eliminated the distance between them and pressed his lips to hers.

Their first kiss had come unexpectedly, and had been

initially tentative, explorative. But this one was bolder and insistent. His firm lips pried hers open. There wasn't any teasing this time just urgent clashing of lips and tongues. His hands cupped her face, and she clutched his trim waist, feeling the solid muscle underneath. He pressed his body into hers, and she felt his erection up against her. Her body responded to it with the beginning of a low thrum all over.

"Jolene," he moaned her name against her mouth and it honestly sounded like a prayer, a benediction, and she wanted to be all that and more for him.

His hands travelled down her body without breaking the kiss. She desperately wanted to feel his touch without the T-shirt hindering the experience. His hands found a home on both of her breasts, and he gave them an appreciative squeeze before he broke their kiss.

He played with the weight of her breasts, filling his hands with them, gently teasing and toying with her nipples through the shirt, drawing them to aching buds. She bit her lip so she wouldn't shout out, but then he lowered his head and took one T-shirt-covered nipple into his mouth, the combination of his hot mouth and the abrasive fabric of her shirt took her to an edge she'd never gone before with just nipple play. She needed him inside her. He played with the nipple till the fabric became completely soaked then gently blew on it. He did the same with the other nipple then finally released her.

"Take your shirt off," he said, his voice rough.

The desire she saw in the depths of his brown eyes took all the air from her lungs, and with shaky hands, she removed her T-shirt. His harsh intake of breath turned the pulse that had begun in her core the minute he kissed her into an ache that needed to be taken care of.

"You're so beautiful," he whispered. His voice had morphed into something unrecognizable.

And his words, even spoken through a lustful haze, made a home in the back of her mind. He dipped his head and caught one of her already hard, wet nipples in his mouth and rolled the other between his fingers.

"Please, Jason," she whimpered. Wetness had already built up between her legs and she throbbed.

He released her nipple with a pop. "What do you want, Jolene?" he asked and moved to her other nipple, giving it a tender bite.

"I want you inside me," she said boldly.

"Which part?" Jason asked as he sucked harder on her nipple.

The new pressure made her throw her head back, submitting to the sensation.

"Which part?" he repeated. And with the back of his hand, he caressed her mound.

"You know which part," she said, breathy and frustrated.

"I want to hear you say it."

God, they would not have a fight now. Unable to resist, she defiantly said, "Your steel rod."

He let go of her nipple for a moment and stood to his full height. He looked down at her, and she saw the smile that tried to press past his lips.

"Or…your dick or cock if that's the filthy language you prefer," she said flippantly.

He did smile, then, a crooked and devilish smile, and he followed it up with deliciously painful tugs on her nipples. He lowered his mouth to her ear. "I suspect," he said, guiding her hand to his dick where it strained against his pants, "you'd have no problem screaming for my dick when it's buried inside your tight, little pussy."

Dear God. Hearing those words come out of Jason's mouth had Jolene battling a wave of dizziness. This couldn't be real. But it had to be, because he continued to lazily move her hand up and down his length. The thick vein running on the underside of his dick pulsed, seemingly intent on drawing every last particle of air from Jolene's lungs.

"But unfortunately"—he removed her hand from him —"tonight I won't get to hear you beg for it. We don't have any condoms."

She desperately clutched at his biceps then and tempered a wail of disappointment. She must have been some sort of ruthless mercenary in a past life. What other explanation could there be? The universe had decided to punish her by denying her an orgasm she knew in her gut would be one of the best she ever had. He couldn't leave her like this: needing, so desperately needing.

He gave her collarbone kisses and chuckled against her skin. "Don't worry. I'm still going to make you come. It just won't be with my cock," he said. "That will have to come later."

Later?

He gently guided her to the open door of the bathroom and pushed her up against the doorjamb. She almost made a tepid joke about them not using the perfectly good bed, but then he removed his shirt. Words evaded Jolene as her hands automatically skimmed the slabs of muscle on Jason's arms, and she briefly traced his tattoo.

He dropped to his knees. "Spread your legs."

Any obstinacy she had previously wanted to display fled away at the command. She did what he said, and a harsh sound escaped Jason. He moved his fingers along her folds. Those damn fingers worked her wetness up and down.

They lightly teased her clit till she deliriously moaned his name. "Jason."

"Is your pretty pussy wet for me, Jojo?"

Soft airy sounds escaped Jolene's mouth before Jason hooked her right leg over his left shoulder and pushed her other leg to the side. She couldn't hide here. She was completely and utterly exposed to his gaze, his touch, and she shivered with anticipation as he breathed on her just before his mouth finally pressed onto her sex. She almost collapsed, but his hands held her fast.

His tongue parted her lips and twirled around her clit, lapping her wetness. He moved his tongue in and out of her opening before he finally took a hold of the sensitive button and covered it with his entire mouth, sucking and toying with it. Jolene held onto the doorframe and focused on her body falling apart. That was all she could do.

She was thrown, however, when she caught the image of them in the cheap, full-length mirror that hung against the front door on the opposite side of the room. She barely recognized the desire she saw on her own face, so blatant and raw. Jason kneeled at her feet and did the things he did to her, and at some point along the way he had also released his erection from his pants and now jerked himself off with long, lazy strokes. Energy coursed through her, and when he added a new dynamic by sliding a finger inside of her, it pushed her dangerously close to the edge.

"Come for me," he moaned against her as he added another finger.

The simple prompt did it for her. Jolene screamed and grabbed his hair as he continued to pump his fingers in and out of her until she was hurled into an orgasm that was all light. Her body shook, but he refused to let go of her clit. The two fingers that were inside of her continued to move, and before she could recover from her first orgasm another one came calling. He released her clit once she came for the second time, gently blowing on and caressing her as she recovered.

"I—" she said, trying to formulate words after an orgasm that she was sure shifted the tectonic plates of the earth.

Only after a couple breaths did she notice that Jason still stroked himself. But this time faster and harder. He stood, bracing himself against the doorjamb behind her, caging her in as he buried his face in the crook of her neck and moaned inarticulate words. She didn't want to disrupt his rhythm by attempting to take over, so she rolled his nipples between her fingers and ran her fingernails down his back.

He hissed as she made contact. "Just like that, baby," he said.

He went still as she increased the pressure with which she touched him.

"Fuck. Fuck, Jolene. I'm coming."

He quickly snatched up the pajama bottoms that had pooled around his ankles and released against the fabric, and Jolene pouted, somewhat disappointed that he hadn't finished somewhere on her body. But she wasn't about to complain about something like that after what she'd just experienced. Jason hunched over for a few moments before he straightened and looked at her and smiled.

Her breath caught.

She assured herself it was the residuals of her orgasm and watching him come.

"That was great," he said. A shiver passed through his body as Jolene continued to lightly skim his back with her fingertips.

Jolene could only muster a weak laugh.

"You're tired." He stared into her face.

"I don't stay up late often, and it's three a.m. and you just—" She gestured with her hand.

He raised his eyebrows and gave her a cocky grin. "Made you come really hard?"

She rolled her eyes and averted her gaze. She wasn't embarrassed, but that high had left her exposed and vulnerable. Her brain currently tried to connect the dots she had thrown at it. A day ago, she would've gladly avoided him if she'd bumped into him at a grocery store.

He picked up his T-shirt, since hers had the two wets spots where her nipples would be, and pressed it into her hands. "Go to bed. I'm just going to clean up."

She quickly put the T-shirt on, and got into their bed. She didn't relax, however, until Jason climbed into the bed as well. She actively fought against the expectation that formed in her mind that Jason would wrap his arms around her. She actually preferred it this way. No confusion of what they had just done. Besides, why would anyone want to be burdened with a body clambering all over them throughout a hot, spring night?

"Can I hold you?" Jason asked shyly.

She almost turned into dust at the request. Of course, 1000 percent yes. She would give up tiramisu for the chance.

"Yes, but I can't promise you I won't drool on you."

He hauled her to him, and her back pressed firmly against his chest. He now wore swimming shorts that rubbed roughly against her skin, but he, mercifully, didn't have a shirt on. His one arm and leg circled around her, pulling her farther into his space.

"I literally can still taste you on my lips. I think I'll be fine."

She made a choking sound.

He laughed. "Good night, Jojo."

"Good night."

A good night, indeed. One of the best sleeps she ever had.

Chapter 9

JASON AND JOLENE were in the laundry room attached to the motel, picking up the clothes they'd washed and dried first thing in the morning. They'd been awake since six a.m., and they'd made calls to their respective workplaces and visited the police station. The lead investigator on their case had nothing new to report but reiterated that once the thieves sold the stolen items, locating them would become more difficult.

Jolene threw their dry clothes and underwear into a canvas bag, frustration over their bad luck evident in her movements. Jason's eye caught sight of the T-shirt that Jolene had worn to sleep last night. The image of her stretching in bed early that morning as the sunlight caressed her skin sprang into his mind. They'd acted pleasantly toward one another, and there was no tension or embarrassment between them. However, the little itch of disappointment he experienced over seeing no expectations behind her eyes surprised him.

He told himself it was a good thing. They both knew

last night happened because they needed to exorcise the tension that had built up between them. And though he'd promised there would be another time for them to explore their sexual chemistry, he no longer knew if that was a good idea. What happened in Gregory Lake stayed in Gregory Lake, and they had to leave today. So, any desire he had to pick up a pack of condoms didn't matter.

"I can't believe we're just leaving," Jolene said.

"We have no choice." He ran his hands through his hair. "I'm missing work and volunteering today. I can't miss tomorrow. I have patients who're expecting me."

"God, I know. I know." She let out a frustrated sigh. "There's only so much I can do when I'm out of the office."

She joined him on the tiny bench he sat on. "I have to let Nicky and Ty know what's going on."

A hint of sadness came through in her voice, and she stared blankly at the gyrating washing machine in front of her that cleaned someone else's clothes.

"We'll tell them together. Maybe after lunch," he said.

She turned to him, then. "Don't think I've forgotten you owe me a lobster."

"I don't think the Hive Diner sells lobster."

"Hmm. We can always go somewhere—"

"They might have some canned tuna, though."

The gloom in her was gone now, and her big laugh filled the small space. The sound curled around him.

"You cheap bastard."

With all the drama they had to contend with, Jolene wasn't feeling all that hungry when she and Jason arrived at the

Hive Diner, but she wanted to cash in on her winnings. He wasn't going to get off that easy.

"I'm going to miss this place," she said once they were seated. She looked around the restaurant.

"We've only been here three times," Jason said.

She ignored him and pointed to a particularly quirky painting of a cowboy astride a horse. "A masterpiece I've just now noticed."

Jason peered at the painting over his shoulder and curled his lips in distaste. "Your judgement is questionable."

Rowena arrived at their table with a smile on her face. It wasn't one that reached her eyes or anything, but it encouraged Jolene to divulge the dare she'd won last night at the pub. She made a big show of ordering the most expensive thing on the menu, a seventeen-dollar baked lasagna with extra garlic bread on the side.

"We're also heading out today," Jolene said after Rowena collected their menus.

"Did you end up figuring out what happened to your things?"

"No leads, unfortunately," Jolene said.

"Hmm. Sorry about that."

"But the authorities will be in contact with any developments," Jason added.

Jolene frowned at Jason. He'd given Jolene such a hard time about talking about "their business," and now he did the same thing.

"Okay," Rowena replied. "Well, I hope they find the rest of your belongings."

"Thanks—"

"Why would you say, 'the rest of your belongings'?" Jason asked.

"What?"

Jolene gave him a confused look as well.

"You said you hoped we find the *rest* of our belongings, implying that we have some of them. But why did you assume the thieves didn't take everything?"

"Jason," Jolene said.

Rowena stared at him for a long time. "I don't know what you're implying or why you're interrogating me, but I don't appreciate it."

Jolene grabbed his forearm from across the table, stopping him from saying anything further. "Rowena, I'm sorry. We had three hours of sleep. He's being ridiculous. Thank you so much for your help with everything. We'll take our lunch to go if that's possible."

Rowena eyes stayed trained on Jason. "Sure."

"What's wrong with you?" Jolene hissed once Rowena left.

"I don't trust her. You're the only one who's allowed to act on their suspicions?"

"No, but you also don't insult the people who handle your hair, eyebrows, or food. You could've waited till our meals arrived before throwing accusations."

"I didn't accuse her of anything."

"Yeah, your weird Sherlock Holmes deduction did that for you."

He shrugged.

"Also, you're being hypersensitive over slip-ups. The woman wished us luck and you threw it back in her face. You better tip her really well."

He gave her a skeptical look.

"Your food." Rowena came back with their lunch in plastic bags, practically slamming them onto the table.

"Thank you so much, Rowena, and again I apologize for Jason's rudeness."

"Whatever." Old Rowena had officially returned. "You can pay at the front."

Once they left the diner and were far enough from any wandering eyes, Jolene dumped the plastic bags in a trashcan.

"We'll have to stop somewhere else for lunch," he said.

She squinted and looked at him. "Ya think?"

Chapter 10

"Hi, Nicky, before you say anything, you're on speaker. Jason is with me."

"Hi, Nicole," Jason said.

"Hey, you guys. Is the van good now? This is what happens when I use sketchy rental services. I'm sorry for all the hassle this has caused you two."

"Yes. Nicky about that…" Jolene glanced at Jason. His eyes were focused on the road in front of them. They had picked up their belongings at the motel and checked out. And were now making their way to a supermarket to get some food for the road. They wouldn't stop for the rest of the six-and-a-half-hour journey.

"The truck did break down, but the mechanics repaired it the first day it arrived." She took a breath. She hated the sick feeling in her gut that erupted. Over the years her family, especially her sister, had been a support system that she'd relied on to get through the tough times, and it crushed Jolene to know she'd failed her sister.

"Someone stole a lot of the furniture from the truck

while it was parked overnight on the side of the road," Jason finished for her.

No one said anything for a moment.

Jolene's stomach rolled again. "Nicky. I'm so sorry. Okay? I'll replace the stuff that's missing."

"*We'll* replace them," Jason said.

"What do you mean by a lot?"

Jason pulled up to a supermarket and turned off the van once he found an appropriate parking space.

"The mattress, the rug, the vanity, the lamps, the side tables, and the television," Jolene said, reading from their copy of the police report. "But we're going to replace them all."

Her sister let out a disbelieving laugh. "Someone beat you to the rug."

"I'm sorry," Jolene said again, then she rambled on about her connections to a good independent furniture store in the city.

Earlier that morning, she and Jason had gone through the store's online catalogue. Jolene would call Tessa, the store owner, once she got back home.

"Jojo, calm down," her sister said, interrupting her rapid speech. "Everything is replaceable, and you guys had no choice but to leave the truck out there. Ty and I should have done a more thorough inspection of the van and the company."

"Regardless, I'm sorry."

"Yes, I'm sorry as well, Nicole," Jason said. "We'll make it right."

"We have warranties on some of the things, so before you guys start going overboard, let's talk about it when you arrive."

Jason silently signaled to Jolene and left the van without further comment.

"Jojo, I'm serious. Please don't beat yourself up for this."

"Girl, don't spare my feelings."

"Don't worry about that. You're your own worst critic."

Her sister spoke truthfully, but she wasn't about to dive into those complexities.

They were silent for a time before Nicky asked, "Is Jason still in the van with you?"

"No," she replied tentatively.

"Sooo?" her sister asked.

"So what?"

"How have you two been getting along?"

Jolene looked in the van's side mirror to the front of the supermarket. A steady stream of people walked in and out of the store.

"Jojo, tell me you guys haven't been arguing this entire trip."

"Not exactly."

"What does that mean?"

"Well." Jolene tried to find a tactful way of telling her sister that she let her husband's best friend, a man she could not stand just two short days ago, go down on her. But each possible explanation ended with her sister asking questions that Jolene didn't know she could answer right now.

She looked out at the side mirror again. "He's not as annoying and uptight as I thought."

"That's good."

She knew her sister expected her to expand on what exactly had made her come to that conclusion, but Jolene refused to say anything.

"Jolene Tiffany Baxter."

Shit.

"What?"

"You slept with him!"

"No."

"Yes, you did. You're always forthcoming with details. Especially about how you feel about Jason."

"No," she said, unable to stop the grin that crept onto her face, "he just went down on me."

"Oh my God. Wait. How did this happen? When did this happen? Was it good?"

Her sister essentially screamed into the receiver, and at first it concerned Jolene because her sister wasn't the squealing type. She also thought for sure the entire parking lot could hear her. She quickly took the phone off speaker and pressed the cell phone to her ear.

"It's a long story—"

"Is that a euphemism? Wait. Don't tell me that. There's probably some rule out there that says you can't ask for details about your husband's best friend's penis."

"Nicky, I can't do this right now," Jolene said through a laugh.

"Oh no, we're doing this right now. Because you won't pick up your phone and you won't text me until God knows when."

"I'm seeing you in a few hours. I'll fill you in then. But you can't tell Ty."

A too-long pause followed. "Nicky."

"Okay, okay."

Jolene took one more look in the side mirror, expecting to see a familiar scene at the entrance of the supermarket, instead she saw a usually composed and stoic Jason flailing his arms. He shouted something and ran toward their vehicle.

"Do you guys like each other now? Is that a thing?" her sister asked.

But the odd image of a frantic Jason distracted Jolene. Half a dozen thoughts ran simultaneously through her head. Had the store run out of her favorite brand of potato chips? Had the moving van become a getaway vehicle? She wasn't about that Bonnie and Clyde life. God, was the van about to explode? She panicked a bit and pushed the passenger door open to catch what Jason shouted.

"The red truck! The red truck!"

Her mind tried to decipher what that meant, failing to do it in the process. Had they come up with a secret code she just couldn't remember?

"What?" she anxiously shouted back, halfway out of the van now.

He pointed to a place behind her. She turned and saw a red truck leaving the supermarket they currently were in front of. It had a large eggshell white vanity tied down with harsh yellow rope.

Her sister's vanity table.

"Oh my God."

"Jolene, what's happening?" her sister's voice escaped the cell phone.

"Nicky, I'm going to have to call you back. Love you." She hung up before she could hear her sister's reply. Jason slid into the driver's seat, dumped the things he had purchased in between them. She had only a few moments to resituate herself on her own seat and close the door before Jason backed the van up.

"It turned left at the intersection," she said.

Jason maneuvered out the parking lot and followed the truck down the street. The heavy traffic made the intersection they needed to turn left on impassable, and under her breath, Jolene chanted, "Turn. Turn. Turn."

"Hey, Jolene, we won't catch up to them if we get Tboned," he said in a conversational tone, but she detected a hint of panic.

They had a lead, a lead that came in the nick of time. She needed to at least get that damn vanity table. He eventually had room to turn. At this point the truck bobbed in and out of sight with several cars blocking it.

"I can barely see it," she said, propping up on her knees on the seat. Jason looked at her quickly.

"Put on your seat belt."

"We won't be able—"

"Put on your seat belt."

She begrudgingly sat down and fastened her seat belt. Once seated, Jason jerked the wheel hard to the right and whizzed through the traffic, honking the horn to clear the lane.

"Watch out!" she said, grabbing the roof handle as Jason swerved out of the way of a vehicle just to overtake another.

Though she had lost at least five minutes off her life, they were two cars behind their target vehicle. If she weren't so anxious about catching their thief, she might have been slightly turned on.

They followed the truck for several miles, each silent and brooding as if they were on some high-stakes mission in an espionage movie. The red truck pulled into a neighborhood that appeared ordinary. It wasn't touristy or even lively like the hub they had quarantined themselves in for the last two days. They pulled up to identical town houses lined up one after the other.

Jolene jumped out of the van before Jason could turn off the engine and ran toward the truck that held one of her sister and brother-in-law's furniture.

"Excuse me. Excuse me!" Jolene screeched across the

expanse of the driveway at the middle-age couple that exited the truck.

The two men turned around, both looking bewildered that some woman they'd never seen in their lives ran at full speed toward them.

Jolene arrived in front of them trying to perform elegance she didn't feel. "Sorry to interrupt you both on this"—she took a big intake of air, and made a general motion toward the unremarkable sky—"lovely Monday, but that vanity in the back of your truck. Where did you get it?" She took pride in sounding calm and not keeling over. Slowly, she moved her hands from her knees to her hips.

One of the men, an Asian man with a beard and a bald head, hooked his arm around his partner's waist, and smiled. "We got it at that big secondhand store in Barnaby Plaza."

Jason had shown up by this time, also doing his best casual-inquiry stance.

"Really good selection of home décor and furniture right now," the other man added.

Jason and Jolene looked at one another.

"We ask because two days ago our moving van broke down," Jason began.

Chapter 11

"It was probably a random person who'd driven past the truck and saw an opportunity. It also explains why they didn't take every single thing," Jolene said.

Jolene and Jason sat in Constable Derrick's office, the officer who'd written up their initial complaint. They faced her desk in two mismatched chairs. The clock mounted in front of them ticked loudly and lent the room an unnerving quality. But the ambience complemented the metaphorical tin-foil hats fixed on both of their heads.

"Think about it, though," Jason said. "The latch wasn't broken or damaged. Someone knew how to disengage it without wrecking the truck. The road wasn't busy. What are the chances that one of the few people who *did* pass it, knew how to open the latch without actually destroying the van?"

"I don't know."

Jason reached over to grab a handful of potato chips from the bag on Jolene's lap.

"Someone"—he shoved some chips into his mouth

—"like a mechanic, for example, would know how to open it."

Jolene dusted the residue left on her fingers from the chips and looked at Jason. "You're not seriously thinking that Joey the mechanic stole our stuff?"

"Not just him. Who became super accommodating once she found out we had valuables in the van and then suggested we specifically see Joey?"

"No," Jolene said, but it came out sounding more like a question. "No," she repeated more emphatically.

Jason raised his eyebrows.

Jolene went silent for a few seconds. "Shit."

The door to the office opened. Jolene and Jason straightened in their seats.

"Sorry for the wait," Constable Derrick said. She took a seat at her desk and studied the papers she'd brought with her. "All right. So, we've been able to locate the majority of the items on the list you provided. And fortunately, there won't be a return delay. You can pick up the items immediately once we're done here."

Jolene let herself relax, loosening her grip on the chip bag. Everything would be okay.

"We have two suspects," Constable Derrick said as she turned the paper on her desk to read the back. "An Olivia Pratt—"

The name didn't ring a bell, so Jason's little theory didn't seem likely.

"And a Simon McCarthy," the constable continued.

Jason turned to face Jolene. "Simon. The clerk at the mechanic shop, his name's Simon."

Jolene's heart sank. She shook her head. "How do you remember that?"

"Yes, Mr. McCarthy is a front desk clerk at the mechanic shop that you visited. His girlfriend is a waitress at the Hive Diner. What probably happened was one of them overheard you were traveling with big-ticket items. We think that the actual robbery happened while the van was waiting to be processed at the shop. It was a crime of opportunity."

Jolene's face grew hot, and her stomach churned uncomfortably. She didn't dare look at Jason. She suspected he focused on the constable's words too closely to have a smug expression, but he had to be feeling vindicated in his assessment of her talkativeness. The silver lining, the only thing that prevented Jolene from wallowing in guilt, was that a lot of the items had been found.

"Sorry your stay in Gregory Lake wasn't totally pleasant. Don't let that stop you from visiting again, though," Constable Derrick said.

The constable dealt with the final paperwork, and Jolene and Jason were left to repack the moving van with the returned items. The only things missing were the pair of lampshades and the rug Jolene had coveted. Once they completed that task, she got into the driver's seat and they began the last six hours of their journey.

"I appreciate you not making me feel worse than I already do about accusing Rowena and Joey," Jason said after some time.

Jolene briefly turned to look at him. "And I appreciate that you haven't brought up the fact that this was my fault."

"Oh, I will." He laughed. "But you're driving, and I'm trying to actually make it to our destination this time."

She jerked the steering wheel a little bit, and she grinned when he gripped the chair.

Ty and Nicole greeted them at their new home with drinks and baked goods that Ty, thankfully, didn't make. After a quick tour of the house, Jason found Jolene standing on her sister's new porch looking into the untidy and weed-ridden backyard. She acknowledged his presence with a smile, and they watched in silence as the sun dipped behind the houses. The last leg of their trip had been bless-edly uneventful, but an odd sense of accomplishment mingled with their exhaustion as they drew closer and closer to their destination. Jason experienced something eerily close to disappointment, like a kid leaving a sleep-over too early.

Jason felt silly, but he knew the feelings were temporary, and he'd return to his routine where Jolene was but a person he tangentially knew. It was for the best, anyway. He was busy, she was busy, and though they survived being in each other's presence for a few days, they weren't well-suited for long-term friendship.

"The takeout is here," Nicole shouted from her new kitchen.

The four of them congregated around the island to eat.

"We need details," Nicole said.

Jolene shrugged. "We messed up, we fixed it, and now we're here."

"Riveting," Ty said.

Jolene laughed and relented, giving more information about their detour. She obviously didn't talk about them being intimate, but Jason didn't expect to feel pleased when she also didn't divulge other details like their karaoke night or free cinnamon buns. He liked the idea of having little and trivial things that only they knew about.

They all went to bed soon after dinner. Sleeping on an air mattress didn't give Jason the most sound of sleeps, but he and Jolene were up early the next morning at the airport to catch their separate flights.

"I didn't hate this trip as much as I thought I would, so thank you," he said as they diverged to their separate gates.

She laughed and playfully slapped his arm. "See you around."

Chapter 12

"Jojo, the meeting is starting in ten minutes." Yvonne, an account manager and her best friend, poked her head into her office.

Jolene started at the sudden intrusion and slammed her phone facedown into her desk.

"Sorry, I didn't mean to interrupt your lunch break," Yvonne said, eyeing Jolene's phone as she came into the office. A pair of glasses sat on her head as her signature ponytail swung like a switch behind her. "I just assumed you'd be working through it like you usually do."

"No, it's okay. And I was working. Kind of."

"Sure. So, anyone interesting you've matched with recently?"

Jolene had signed up for a dating app two weeks ago. She intended to keep it private. Her own tepid reintroduction into the dating scene, but Yvonne had seen the app on her phone and now felt invested in her romantic happiness. Jolene wasn't even sure if she wanted a full-fledged relationship yet. But she was horny and refused to deal with the men she worked with.

"Why do you assume I was swiping through candidates?" Jolene asked as she walked to her office door and scanned the hallway for any eavesdroppers. She shut it and turned toward her friend.

"Because you had that look on your face that's pensive but also slightly disturbed?"

Jolene let out an exhausted sigh.

"So?" Yvonne sat on the edge of Jolene's desk and played with a paperweight. Her cigarette trousers and billowy dress shirt made her look like a chic pirate.

"No. Why is everyone in this city obsessed with tapas? I'd also appreciate conversations that don't revolve around the same three TV shows. Also, dick pics. So many unwanted dick pics."

"So, I'm guessing you haven't gone out with anyone, then."

Jolene scrunched up her face. "No, but for a second, I thought I'd accidentally matched with Mark, but it turned out to be a random guy who looked eerily like him."

Mark was a man who ran in their professional circles.

"Girl, eliminate the look-alike and the weirdos who send pictures of their penises and give the ones who are mildly interesting and attractive a chance. Most people don't shine over text."

Jolene didn't say anything because of course that was the most logical next step. And she had a few conversations going on with a couple men that weren't completely horrible.

"Unless you have a person in mind, and all these guys are just placeholders," Yvonne said.

"Subtle."

It had been five weeks since her trip with Jason, and she had been unable to shake off the feeling she missed him. It was ridiculous, but it explained why she found herself thinking about him or what he might be doing at a particular moment. She would catch herself doing it and silently scold herself and then fall into doing it again a few hours later. She'd told Yvonne about their night in the motel room, and what should have been a blip on her sexual experience chart had become a talking point whenever love, sex, and relationships came up.

"You know how I feel. Call him and put yourself out of this misery," Yvonne said, pointing to Jolene's phone.

The look on Jolene's face made Yvonne laugh.

"Even if I were to go against every instinct in my body and call him, I don't want to date anyone right now."

"Well, who said anything about dating? You might not be ready now, but you'll eventually want a relationship, and why should you not have fun in the meantime?"

Jolene actually mulled over it. "What would I say? 'Hey Jason, it's Jolene. I haven't stopped thinking about having sex with you. Wanna do it again?'"

"Yeah, why not?"

Well, first, the thought of proposing such a thing and Jason swiftly rejecting her sounded like just the thing to further delay her reentrance into the dating scene. Her marriage had been one of the first things in her life that she'd committed to without reservations or outside pressure. When it ended, her confidence had been shaken. It felt like she'd trusted the ground beneath her feet only for it to crack and engulf her in a cavern of heartbreak and shame. She never wanted to experience that again. So, she couldn't repeat old habits; she had to be more judicious during the dating process.

"Okay, this is getting too involved for a Tuesday afternoon," Jolene said as she grabbed her tablet and coffee mug and walked out of her office. "We're going to be late."

She and Yvonne walked the long hallways before

entering a small boardroom where an intern already sat. The clients, the two owners of the apothecary line, were just taking their seats.

"Jolene," Jessica, part owner of Essential Essence Apothecary, immediately said as she leapt from her seat before she and Yvonne could fully enter the room. "You told me these trolls would leave me alone once I apologized and donated money to that anti-bullying thing. It's been weeks and they're still all over my ass on social media."

"Good afternoon, Jessica"—Jolene looked at the other owner seated next to Jessica appearing decidedly anxious —"Carmen."

Carmen responded with an apologetic smile and nod.

"Well?" Jessica asked, still standing as if she might launch herself across the table if Jolene didn't provide her with a good enough response.

"Jessica," Jolene said in the same tone one might use to coax a terrified animal from its hiding place. "As I said before, the social media heat is unlikely to go away completely, but the most important thing is to—"

"Not respond, I know. But how the hell am I supposed to promote anything when people keep spamming my social media pages with pasta emojis?"

The video of Jessica completely going off on a waitress who had delivered a wrong order, a linguini rather than a risotto, wasn't flattering. It had shown Jessica getting unnecessarily loud, threatening to withhold a tip from the waitress, and "accidentally" spilling her glass of water onto the table. Folks had been angry and had gone to social media wielding their pasta emojis and written disapproval to mock and admonish Jessica and by extension, Essential Essence.

Jolene herself had been more than tempted to down-size the planned campaign when she finally watched the video. Jessica had already proven to be a difficult client even before the fiasco. She didn't trust Jolene's expertise and questioned her every step of the way. But Carmen, the sweet second half of the business, had begged them not to change their plans. Carmen had invested so much into the business, and even sitting here, she sent apologetic glances and smiles on behalf of her saboteur who happened to be her childhood friend and business partner.

"All right, Jessica. You're only to go onto your personal social media when either Erin"—Jolene pointed to the intern—"or I give you preplanned posts."

After the meeting that included drafting Carmen and Jessica's vision for their launch party at the beginning of September, Jolene and Yvonne walked their clients out. Jolene smiled and waved goodbye when they entered the elevator, and she bit down the sarcastic comment she wanted to make under her breath.

"You're still coming to spin class with me this week, right?" Yvonne asked. They stopped at the junction between their offices. Yvonne's girlfriend, Diana, had been called in as the understudy last minute for an opera role. It was fantastic, but that meant she had flown east to Montreal to fulfill the role. It left Yvonne without anyone to go to the last week of a six-week program she'd found on Groupon.

Jolene sent her friend a weary side-glance. "The loud music and strobe lights are going to give me harrowing flashbacks to my early twenties."

"Ha, so I guess this week is about reintroductions in more ways than one."

It was a Saturday afternoon, and Jolene had found her way

outdoors to do some shopping at the local farmer's market. Yesterday, she'd regained full range of motion in her legs after a brutal spin class, and she'd decided to celebrate by picking up some produce she promised herself she would use in a recipe she didn't have yet.

Jolene studied some onions for a moment before putting a couple in her canvas bag. A gentle tap on her forearm drew her attention. A short, brown-skinned woman in her sixties stood beside her. Her white hair had been cut into an edgy bob, and she wore a large straw visor.

"Could you grab those leeks for me, love?" The older woman sweetly smiled and pointed to the vegetables just out of her reach. She had a slight accent that Jolene couldn't place.

"Oh, for sure," Jolene said, handing two to the woman.

"Thank you." The woman smiled up at her. "You look so familiar."

Jolene had never seen this woman in her life, but she smiled and shrugged, not knowing exactly how to respond.

The woman turned her head and called out, "Elizabeth."

Another woman in her sixties emerged from the makeshift aisles of the farmer's market. She stood slightly taller and slimmer than the plump woman before her, but she wore an identical straw visor. Her dress had a lovely floral detail across the neckline. Jolene inwardly groaned, knowing from experience with the aunties in her family that she could expect to be subjected to intense analysis until the two figured out why she looked like a particular person they knew. But before she could come up with a polite way to extricate herself from the situation, another person rounded the corner close behind the woman in the dress.

"Jason," Jolene said. Her heart rattled within the confines of her chest, jarred by the sudden appearance of the man who had occupied her thoughts for the last five weeks. How could one person be that handsome? He dressed much in the same way he had the last time she'd seen him, casual and hot as hell.

"Jason, you know her?" the woman with the cool haircut asked.

If Jolene hadn't been staring at him so intently, she wouldn't have seen the way his eyes had widened.

"Mom, this is Nicole's sister, Jolene. The one I drove with when I helped Ty and Nicole move last month."

The two women turned to Jolene with their mouths open in silent *O*s.

"Yes, yes. Of course," Jason's mother said, studying Jolene's face and smiling.

Jolene was stuck. Her mind played a relay of table tennis as it tried to pinpoint the appropriate thing to say in this situation. She had the unnatural urge to tell Jason she had thought about him a lot. But Jolene knew, like she knew pale pink was not her color, admitting that would be the worst thing to say in this situation.

"And Jolene this is my mother, Nadine, and my aunt, Liza."

"It's nice to meet you," Jolene said, shaking both older women's hands. She tried to infuse all the charm she could possibly muster into the handshakes. She now felt invested in these women's opinions of her.

"We're going to get lunch if you want to join us," Aunt Liza said with the same gentle Tongan accent as Jason's mother. And though she wanted to scream yes, she could already feel the protest that rose from Jason's body.

"I'm sure Jolene has better things to do on a Saturday

afternoon, Elizabeth," Jason's mother said, still staring intently at Jolene.

"Oh, you would think so," Jolene said. Why did she make herself sound that pathetic? "What I mean is I wouldn't want to intrude."

"I'm inviting you, so you wouldn't be intruding," Aunt Liza continued.

"Auntie, she might not want to join us," Jason said, looking more than a little uncomfortable.

Did he think she wanted to worm her way into his life because he gave her two of the best orgasms she ever experienced?

"Then let her say that."

Jolene gave an apologetic smile. "I can't stay. I actually have a few more boring errands to run today." She did in fact have things to do, but she couldn't tell if Jason's shoulders slumped in relief or in disappointment.

Jason's mom pursed her lips. "Then come for dinner next Friday evening."

Jolene's felt her heart rate spike and palms dampen. Could she spend an entire evening having polite conversation with Jason's family? Was there any need to complicate her emotions? What if he really didn't want her there and he bemoaned his mother's involvement?

"Sure," she said, not thinking about the possible responsibilities that might conflict with this new obligation.

"Fantastic," Aunt Liza said.

"Great!" Jolene replied a little too enthusiastically.

Jason's mother hooked her arm through Aunt Liza's. "Jason, give her my address." The two women turned to leave. "We'll see you at six, love," Jason's mom said over her shoulder.

They disappeared into the busy market and left Jolene and Jason alone. He drew closer to her and just stood there. "You might want to write this down," he said with a small smile.

Jesus.

She pulled out her phone, and he recited his mother's address.

"I don't have to come if you don't want me to," Jolene said, putting her phone away.

"Why wouldn't I want you to?"

"I'm not trying to encroach on your life."

"It's dinner with my family, that's it. You're my best friend's sister-in-law; it makes sense that we'd be at least friendly to one another."

More than friendly would be preferable. Memories flooded back of their time in the motel room.

He interrupted her thoughts with a polite cough. "I should go find my mother and aunt before they decide that their next project will be harvesting live lobster. I'll see you next Friday, then."

"It's a date."

Crap, Jolene cursed inwardly.

"Not a date, date. But like a—"

"Yeah, I-I know what you meant."

"Good, because I don't want you thinking you went down on a woman one time and here she is wanting a date." Lights and the *Kill Bill* siren went off in her head telling her to stop talking.

His eyes narrowed and a smile curved his lips. "You still think about it, don't you?"

"You arrogant bastard," she said almost breathlessly.

He shrugged. "I just know my skill level."

And as he walked farther and farther away from her, she felt a knot in her stomach form. She was in trouble.

Chapter 13

JASON HAD BEEN on edge the entire week. That wasn't a good thing when you dealt with teeth and drills and people who were often afraid of them. Tonight, Jolene would come over to his mother's for dinner, and Jason couldn't help but count down the minutes till work ended.

He'd thrown himself back into his routine during the weeks prior to seeing Jolene again at the farmer's market, and their accidental meeting had rattled him. It shouldn't have, however, because in the back of his head he knew there was a possibility he'd see her out and about in the city, crossing the street downtown or out at dinner with friends.

"Hey, doc, are you coming out with us?" one of the receptionists at the clinic asked.

"No, I have plans already."

The receptionist didn't look surprised. He thought his coworkers would stop inviting him out after several years of him refusing, but he suspected courtesy motivated them to continue to ask on the very unlikely chance he would agree. It wasn't that he didn't like the other dentists, hygienists, or the front staff he worked with. In fact, a lot of them were nice to talk to in the mornings before the first patients arrived, during conferences they attended, or their annual Christmas party he made sure to attend. But Jason found it taxing to spend several hours in a bar, racking his brain for topics to talk about.

However, while he bid his coworkers to have a good weekend, he liked knowing he actually had plans that didn't consist of going to the gym or straight home as he often did on Friday evenings.

The moment he arrived at his mother's home, she greeted him saying, "Jason, don't just stand there; we have a guest arriving soon." She handed him a bowl that held white yams, and he took it to the dining table without protest.

He straightened the four placemats and utensils while he was there. Thankfully, his aunt hadn't brought along his uncle and cousins. If his uncle got the chance, he would only talk about MMT, the Tonga national rugby league team, and it took a very specific set of skills to avoid that conversation. He didn't want Jolene to feel overwhelmed meeting so much of his family at once.

After his mom and aunt had met Jolene, they'd bombarded him with questions about her. It's what happened when you were well into your thirties and an only child. However, he'd let them know immediately that Jolene would not be the one. His mom saw any woman with all her teeth as a potential match, but he didn't indulge in his mother's matchmaking. It would probably be nice to have a long-term partner, maybe a kid or two, but it wasn't something he'd envisioned or thought out like he had with his other goals.

The doorbell rang.

"I'll get it," he called out. He forced himself not to jog

toward the sound, but he couldn't help but walk briskly to the door. When he opened the door, Jolene stood there, like some kind of goddess of nature with bouquets of flowers in each hand.

"Hi," she said. Her voice sounded a little high-pitched and breathy.

"Hi, welcome. Come in."

She shuffled inside and nervously scanned his childhood home from the limited vantage point in the entrance area. A few years after his father passed away, he and his mom were forced to move out, but Jason bought the house back for her once he had become some version of a success. Having Jolene in this space brought on heavy palpitations that Jason attempted to control with even breathing. But the mango-coconut scent had returned and tested his resolve to remain chill. He'd missed that smell.

"I brought flowers for your aunt and mom."

"They'll love them."

"I didn't know what their favorites were, so I just got them mine."

"Oh, Jolene. Welcome."

His mother and aunt appeared in the entryway. As always, his aunt, the quiet observer who communicated mostly with her eyebrows and expressive eyes, smiled at Jolene.

"Are these for us?" his mom asked, reaching out for the two bouquets and cooing over their color and scent. "Elizabeth, they're beautiful, aren't they?"

"Very. I love gardenias. Thank you."

"Jason, put these in vases for us." She passed the bundles to him and turned back to Jolene. "Also, this outfit —" She eyed the black jumpsuit Jolene had worn and gave her a thumbs-up.

Jason also thought she looked great but kept that to himself.

"Tonight, you're going to eat some Tongan food. I hope you're hungry," his mom said.

"This is lu pulu," his mother said, pointing to the dish that had meat, onions, and coconut milk baked in taro leaves.

Jolene leaned in, her eyes wide. "It smells wonderful." She ate with an appetite that spoke to some level of comfort in her environment. It was mesmerizing to watch.

"Jason will have to teach you how to prepare it one of these days. He's a very good cook," his mom said, pride shining through her words.

Jason liked the idea of cooking for Jolene, especially the food he grew up on. The food that he'd hated taking to school in lieu of the peanut-butter-and-jelly sandwiches the rest of his classmates brought.

When Jolene went in for a second helping, his mom asked, "Do you enjoy cooking?"

"Not particularly, but I have to survive somehow," Jolene said drily.

"Yeah, pop and potato chips don't cut it," Jason said.

She turned to him and laughed, throwing her head back. His aunt and mom looked a little confused but didn't ask for any clarification or an explanation. Maybe Jolene's laugh captivated them as much it did him. He shoveled the rest of the food into his mouth, not really tasting much.

"Funny girl," his aunt said as they all cleared the table and packed the leftover food.

He and Jolene moved to the living room together as his aunt and mom rummaged for board games in his childhood bedroom turned storage room.

"You don't have to stay if you don't want to," Jason said.

"I can stay for another hour or so," she replied.

Jason relaxed at her words. He reasoned that he wanted to put off the inevitable questions that would be coming his way once she left.

She took a turn around the living room, stopping in front of prayer candles and picture frames that decorated the mantel and the walls. He sat in a settee facing the fireplace, pretending not to watch her as he scrolled through his email inbox.

"You were a cute kid. You look pissed in each photo I've seen of you, though," she said.

He laughed. "I was a serious child."

She smiled at him over her shoulder. "I can imagine you keeping a strict inventory of your toys or something equally as adorable."

"Nah, mostly I just made my friend remove his shoes before he came into my bedroom. Maybe that's why I only had the one friend." He'd been a loner in his early school years. It wasn't until he grew tall, filled out, and played football in high school that he made friends.

"One is enough, but I bet you had an itinerary for what you would accomplish during play dates."

"My lists are epic; it's not my problem you can't see that."

She shook her head and continued perusing. "Who's this?" she asked, standing in front of a picture at eye level between the TV set and fireplace. He knew immediately which photo she studied.

"My dad."

She turned to him. "You look like him."

He clenched his jaw at the sudden wave of emotions. "I'm glad for that."

"Do you get to see him often?"

"He died when I was ten."

"God. I'm so sorry." She fidgeted with her hands. "I should've remembered. Nicky told me a while back."

"It's all right. We haven't liked each other for very long. I won't hold it against you."

She winced at his attempts to alleviate the tension.

"He was a great father. I still have good memories." He had an urge to tell her all about said memories, but his mom and aunt returned with Scrabble, and that meant conversations about his dad were over.

"'QIS' is so not a word," Jolene said, throwing up her hands.

They'd played for close to an hour and the intensity of the game highlighted the competitiveness that emerged when she dealt with Jason. He placed his phone up into her face, and she read the legitimate definition of a very real word she'd never seen before. She leaned backwards onto her hands and gave him a resigned look.

A smug smile appeared on his face.

"Ms. Elizabeth, it's your turn," Jolene said.

"I only have three tiles left," the older woman said as she studied the hectic board for several minutes.

"Oh, come on, Elizabeth," Ms. Nadine urged. She waved her arms in a shoo motion toward her sister.

Ms. Elizabeth eventually placed a blank tile she'd hoarded for the entire game to the end of a word. "I want that to be an *S*," she said.

"Okay, *now* we can total up our points," Ms. Nadine proclaimed.

It turned out that Jason won by half a dozen points with Ms. Elizabeth right behind him, followed by Jolene.

Jolene smiled at Ms. Nadine. "I guess we'll need to brush up on obscure words." Jolene fought the need to say something petty in regard to Jason's win by being aggressively good-natured. Jason raised his eyebrows as if he knew she fought an internal battle. His family seemed to like her, and she thought poor sportsmanship wouldn't win her any points. Not that she tried to impress Ms. Nadine or Ms. Elizabeth beyond any normal expectations of respect.

"I should go," Jolene said, looking at the time on her phone. "Thank you so much for a fantastic meal and an overall great night."

The two women hugged her and told her she should come back soon, and Ms. Elizabeth promised she would bring her husband and kids for her to meet. Ms. Elizabeth insisted she take a Tupperware of food home.

"Remember to listen to our podcast, and if you're on Facebook, share."

Jason walked her to the door. "That wasn't so bad, was it?"

"Your aunt and mom are the sweetest. But that game of Scrabble has me thinking I was right for believing you're arrogant," Jolene said.

"You're also very competitive."

She shrugged. "You're looking at the three-time spelling bee champion of Wind Pine Elementary School. Spelling is in my blood."

"Holding onto decades-old wins, huh?"

"Hell yes."

The words they might have said after that didn't come. He drew closer, and she could feel his body heat. Her heart rate kicked up a bit, and she could only focus on how much she wanted Jason to kiss her and have those strong arms wrapped around her once again. How could one experience muddle her expectations so much? She wasn't a woman who mooned over men. But she'd been daydreaming about him and his kisses for weeks, to the point where she wasn't sure if she'd overhyped the experience in her mind and misremembered the details.

Then Jason's lips were on hers, and his mouth teased with a level of tenderness that made her feel heated. The kiss was more than what she'd imagined or remembered. She clutched the Tupperware harder in her hands, unwilling to spill its contents right outside the door of Ms. Nadine's home. But in the process of holding the container so tightly, she triggered her car's alarm. The blaring, obnoxious sound brought their kiss to an abrupt end. She fumbled with her car keys that had been wedged between her hand and the container to turn it off. She also tried to get her need under control.

"I should let you go," he said, his voice gruff and barely audible. "Text me when you arrive home safely."

"Okay. Will do."

"Good night."

"Thanks again."

She gave him a nod, he waved, and she drove away with a smile that she only noticed when it grew into a grin.

Chapter 14

ON A GOOD DAY, Jason had ten minutes to scarf down his lunch before his next patient. Today was no different. He took big bites of an apple as he entered the staff room. He stopped momentarily at a notice board to study the new additions of hand-drawn pictures from their young patients.

"I don't know why we bother. He's not going to come," one of the three dentists who worked at the clinic, Cynthia, said.

"That's a good thing," a dental hygienist he often worked with, Marvin, replied. Jason kind of wanted to know whom they talked about, but he generally avoided gossip; still, naturally he was curious. To eliminate any possibility of finding out and inadvertently becoming a part of work drama, he prepared to take another bite into his apple to let the room's occupants know that someone else could hear their conversation.

But before he did so, his colleague spoke. "My eyes glaze whenever he attempts small talk."

The other laughed. "Poor Akana."

Well, shit.

Jason didn't think he was the most exciting person but "glazed eyes"? Not wanting to hear any more insights into his personality, Jason shifted past the wall that hid him from view. Cynthia and Marvin both abruptly changed subjects, unsure whether they'd been heard. Jason smiled at both of them and acted as if he hadn't been eavesdropping.

After work, Marvin approached him. "Hey, Akana, a few of us are getting some drinks if you want to come."

Jason suspected this was Marvin's way of apologizing if Jason had indeed overheard his gossiping during lunchtime.

"No, I'm okay. Have fun."

Marvin looked relieved, and whether it was because Jason wouldn't be joining them or because he detected no animosity on Jason's part, he didn't know. But what Jason did know, was that when he walked to his car and passed his coworkers huddled in a group in front of the clinic as they coordinated their after-work plans, a wave of self-consciousness washed over him for the first time.

He made it through a workout and arrived home, at least knowing that he'd had a productive day. At the front of his apartment building, he met the elderly Ukrainian couple that lived in the building. Whenever they happened to come across one another in the hallways or in the parking lot, Mrs. Bayuk wouldn't fail to mention her granddaughter. Her intentions were clear to anyone within earshot. But if he wasn't even receptive to his own mother's matchmaking attempts, there was no way that he'd potentially wreck a decent neighborly relationship by dating the Bayuk's granddaughter.

"Jason, good evening," Mrs. Bayuk said as she smiled, causing the wrinkles around her eyes and mouth to deepen. Her thick accent made her Ukrainian heritage undeniable.

"Mrs. Bayuk"—he turned to the older man—"Mr. Bayuk."

The older couple complemented each other in appearance. They wore similar colors and stood at similar heights. They looked comfortable next to one another like salt-and-pepper shakers. Jason held the door open for them.

"You are always sweating," Mrs. Bayuk said. She looked him up and down. "It is good. Keeps you big and strong."

He gave her a small smile for the compliment. He ushered them into the elevator and pressed their floor number then his.

"My granddaughter, Bailey, if you recall, likes sports. Tennis and swimming."

He always humored the older woman by listening to her brag about her granddaughter while Mr. Bayuk would stand beside her holding her hand. He didn't look bored or impatient, just resigned to his wife's familiar commentary.

Jason usually dodged any suggestions that he go out with Bailey by claiming busyness at work, but he would placate the older woman by complimenting her jewelry or nail polish. "That's a pretty necklace, Mrs. Bayuk."

The woman blushed and pressed her palm to her chest where the necklace laid, her scheme forgotten. The elevator opened to the older couple's floor, and he waved them goodbye. Jason exited the elevator on his own floor, and it struck him before he could make it to his apartment door that for the second time that day, he'd dodged a potential social outing. It wouldn't have bothered him if he hadn't overheard the comment about him being boring. He tried to recall the last time he'd left his bubble.

The road trip with Jolene.

He frowned.

Upon entering his apartment, he placed his keys in the delegated bowl in the small entryway, removed his sneakers, and headed to the shower. He closed his eyes as the cold water ran down the expanse of his body.

It would be nice if Jolene were here.

His eyes shot open. Jolene had been occupying some of his headspace. Thoughts would cross his mind throughout the day. Most were innocent in nature, but the ones he had in the shower and in bed had him reaching for his cock. And if his day had gone a little differently maybe he would've jerked off and called it a night, but today highlighted that he was a total square.

It wasn't necessarily a bad thing, but he was stagnant for the first time in his life. There wasn't a goal he was grinding or hustling to achieve, and it bothered him. What made his mild listlessness even worse was the blank he drew every time he tried to come up with something to fix it. He needed to reenergize his life. Do something different and out of his comfort zone. Maybe then he'd discover the next goal to strive for or at least find out how to enjoy what he'd already accomplished.

Before he could reason with himself, he got out of the shower, not caring that water dripped all over the carpet. He retrieved his cell phone and pulled up Jolene's contact.

Jason: Hey, Jolene. It's Jason.

Jolene: Hi (you do know I have your name programmed into my phone, right?)

He hesitated. This could be a horrible misstep.

Jason: Do you want to grab coffee sometime this week?

It took her seven minutes to respond, but the answer made the wait worth it.

Jolene: Yes.

He spotted Jolene immediately when he entered the café that sized their drinks in a different language. A young woman with locs took his order, and he made his way to where Jolene sat once he got his drink. They'd planned to meet after work, so Jolene wore a shift dress with a blazer over it. He'd never seen her in work attire, and he liked how she looked in it.

"Hi," Jolene said as she shoved the chair across from her with her foot. "How are you?"

"Good. How's your week going?"

"Honestly? Busy, and I'm ready to rip my hair out."

He quirked his eyebrow and laughed. He'd practiced what he needed to say. All the points he had planned were compelling, and there was a good chance she would be down for it. But there also was a small possibility that she might be offended. They took sips of their drinks and commented on the unusual stretch of sunny weather.

"Okay, not for nothing, but why are we here?" Jolene finally asked.

"We're friends, aren't we?"

"We are?"

"Sure, why not?"

"Well, when you answer like that, you can't blame a girl for questioning."

He smiled. "I'm tired of pretending I don't actually enjoy your company."

She narrowed her eyes "Okay, I can also admit you're mildly amusing."

He'd take it. Jason pulled out his phone. "I also can't really pretend that we don't have chemistry. So I have a proposition—"

"Oh my God, you're going to ask me to be your fuck

buddy." She leaned into the table almost tipping over her coffee mug.

Embarrassed that his intentions were that obvious, Jason looked around uncomfortably. "That's part of it. But I was going to put it more tastefully."

She raised her hands in surrender "Okay, friends-with-benefits."

He scrunched his face. "I don't like that term either."

She smiled. "I guess it doesn't matter what you want to call it. It ends up meaning the same thing."

He lowered his voice a touch. "I just thought that there isn't any real reason why we shouldn't explore what we started in Gregory Lake."

She studied him for a moment. He shifted in his seat, trying to determine if his proposition offended her. He didn't want her to think that he thought of her as a sex object to simply satisfy his need. Instead, with Jolene, he saw the potential to have a fun, sexy, but casual arrangement that both of them would enjoy.

"Well, since we're not pretending anymore, I won't pretend to think about it, and just say yes now," she said.

He heard the words, but they didn't completely register.

"I said, I'm down to do the whole, you scratch my itch and I scratch yours, but I'm not looking for anything permanent or even long-term," she said.

He nodded emphatically. "No feelings. Check. And sleeping with each other exclusively, right?"

"Correct."

"Okay."

He let out a visible sigh of relief and placed his phone back into his pocket.

"You had a list of pros and cons prepared, didn't you?"

How did she know him so well?

"No."

"So much for not pretending."

"Fine. I may have had an entire speech prepared, but you kind of hijacked it."

"Please, it would have taken away any fun from something that's all about having fun."

"So, we have a deal?"

She nodded. "You can even add to your pro side that this arrangement might make this human form you see in front of you, running solely on coffee and sheer spite, less grumpy."

They continued to talk. She went into more detail about her chaotic day, and he told her about the new plants he bought for his place. It was light and buoyant, and there was no further discussion of the logistics of their arrangement, but he was relieved that it was out in the open and that he was going to get Jolene in his bed, and possibly against a wall. And he definitely wanted her in front of a full-length mirror. The possibilities made his pants feel tight.

"Jolene," a woman called across the coffee shop.

"Oh, Yvonne."

A tall woman with light brown skin approached their table. She had a silky ponytail that reached her mid-back. And wore an all red pantsuit. She stood in front of him with her hands in her pockets, assessing Jason behind her glasses.

"Jason, this is my coworker and best friend, Yvonne. Yvonne, this is Jason."

He stood to shake her hand.

She wore a cryptic smile. "Yes, Jason. It's nice to finally meet you. I've heard so much about you."

Jolene coughed.

"Well, it's nice to meet a friend of Jolene's." Realizing

he would be late to meet his mom and aunt, he added, "I should be heading out. I'll text you."

Jolene stood and leaned in as if to hug him. He didn't hesitate to put his arms around her and complete the action. He would've kissed her or given her a peck on the cheek if Yvonne wasn't standing right there watching them. But he left the café and noticed the sun shone brighter and he could pick up a melody or two that some bird sang.

Chapter 15

JOLENE HADN'T ANTICIPATED how difficult scheduling sex with Jason would be. They had been trying for two weeks now. Their busy schedules and her inconsistent plans made everything much more complicated. Wasn't the whole concept of friends-with-benefits supposed to be convenience? They'd had opportunities here and there, but it would've been too similar to the quickies she did in college. This was supposed to be a mature and sensual arrangement. Wasn't it?

Friday evening arrived with yet another failed attempt to schedule anything. It was fine. Everything was fine. She would not focus on the horniness she barely kept at bay. She would spend this Friday like she did most Fridays. After leaving her deserted office building, she drove home and bopped to the music of some local hip-hop artist that blared a little too loudly in her car.

When she arrived home, she dumped her keys and work bags on a table next to the door and kicked her heels off, not seeing exactly where they landed. She thumbed through her mail as she preheated the oven for the thin crust, frozen pizza she had kept for such a moment as this.

She took a quick shower, removed her makeup, and tied a satin headscarf around her hair. She curled up into the corner of her sofa and started the latest episode of *The Real Housewives of Potomac* she'd recorded. She was on her third pizza slice and in the middle of a group text with her mom and sister, recounting the shenanigans unfolding on her screen, when Jason's caller ID popped up on her phone.

She felt a little tremor in her hand as she answered the phone. "Hey." Her greeting was cut off by the piece of pizza that she hadn't fully swallowed going down the wrong pipe.

"You okay?" Jason asked.

Jolene, through the force of her coughing, tried to deflate her own lung. "Yes!" she wheezed at the phone. She placed her cell on the coffee table so as not to diminish Jason's hearing with the harsh, aggressive sound. After what felt like a longer period of time than one would spend in a DMV line, she regained control. While wiping the tears from her eyes and trying to find the dignity the universe withheld from her, Jolene placed the phone to her ear.

"Hi."

"Hi, again. I thought I might have to call for help."

"God, I choked on a piece of pizza. I feel like it would've been on brand for me to go out like that."

He chuckled through the receiver, and the sound, maybe because it was so close to her ear, made her shiver.

"Listen, I just finished playing flag football with the kids from my after-school program, and I don't know if you're at home or busy. But I can come over, if you want?"

"I'm at home and I'm not busy," she said as she stared

at the screen she'd paused in the middle of an argument between the ladies of the show. She tried to sound casual and blasé about it, but her body was already abuzz and ready.

"Great. Your address?"

She gave it to him, and he said he'd be there in twenty. She hung up and just pressed her cell phone to her chest, relieved and giddy that she was finally going to get laid. Then she looked down at what she wore. A bleach-stained T-shirt and a pair of large, cover-your-entire-ass-and-belly-button cotton panties.

She quickly jumped into action, chucking the remaining pizza into her fridge and shoving the shoes that cluttered the entryway to the side to create some sort of path. She lit the candles that decorated her tables and changed into leggings, a bralette with matching panties, and an off-the-shoulder T-shirt that she had paid too much for at an online boutique. She brushed her teeth and decided to forgo makeup, but she removed her headscarf and fluffed up her curls until they were huge and framed her head and face like a massive halo.

Okay, calm down. Maybe I should pull out the wine glasses. He doesn't drink, silly. Shit.

She looked around her room. The bed was made, a miracle really. And all her clothes were put away, another miracle. She'd have to let her mother know her prayers had been working. And before she could stress herself out thinking about how he would view or judge her living space, the apartment's buzzer rang. She let him in, and within a minute he knocked on her apartment door.

The moment Jason stepped into her apartment she felt it shrink. She nervously looked around. "Welcome," she said.

A crooked smile appeared on his face while he took in her space. A duffle bag swung from his hand and he wore workout clothes.

He moved to remove his shoes, and Jolene said, "You don't have to take your shoes off." On second thought, he kind of had to because the image of him fucking her with just his sneakers on made her want to giggle.

He seemed to know it too and removed his shoes anyway. "Your space is very…" he paused, "…bright."

Jolene, trying to see it from his perspective, assessed the deep-blue accent wall on the far right of the room, the coral-and-white patterned sofa, and the numerous paintings and plants that decorated her space. "Thank you?"

"It's nice." He turned to her. "Very you."

Her heart skipped.

"Let me take your bag and jacket," she said before she could say something ridiculous.

She placed his bag in the hallway leading to her bedroom and overcame the impulse to inhale his jacket or capture the heat from it by wrapping it around herself. Instead, like the sensible adult who did not sabotage the good things in her life by being weird, Jolene hung his jacket over one of her kitchen chairs.

"Do you want anything to drink or eat? I can order in something if you haven't had dinner."

"No, I'll just get some water. I ate a couple sandwiches at the game."

She handed him a glass, and he finished it in two big gulps. Was he thirsty, or was he just as nervous as she was? She'd never done this before, this casual sex with a person you actually know, and all of a sudden she didn't know how to act. But she didn't want to make things awkward so she talked, like she always did.

"All right, do you want to do it on top of the counter or against the balcony rails that haven't been swept since last summer?"

The flash she saw in Jason's eye and the way his eyebrows twitched told her that he was totally into her suggestions.

"You cut straight to the chase," he said.

She laughed lightly. "Well, we both know why and what you're here for."

He placed his glass down and moved directly in front of her. He raised his hand as if he were going to touch her face but then placed it at his side. "This is a mutually beneficial arrangement, if it stops working for you in any way, tell me. We'll adjust or end it."

"Like clownfish and anemone."

A smile tugged at his lips. She wanted his full-blown smile in her direction. The random high school science knowledge about symbiotic relationships hadn't gotten her as close as she wanted.

"I don't want to know what I am in that analogy."

"I'm totally the clownfish. So that would make you the anemone."

Okay what now? Should she lean in and kiss him? Should she talk about how distractingly horny she'd been for the last few weeks?

"Can I take a quick shower? I'm sweaty from running around a field for an hour."

Oh, she didn't mind him being sweaty. She actually—

"Yeah, sure." She led him to the bathroom adjacent to her bedroom. "You can use everything except my hair conditioner."

"No conditioner. Got it."

He shut the door, and she was left to pace her living room and rethink her sex appeal. Her head and body hummed, and she thought she might explode with anticipation. Then a big crash escaped from the bathroom.

"Jason?" she called out.

No answer. *Crap.*

She knocked on the bathroom door. "Jason, I heard a loud bang. Are you okay?"

A muffled answer came but nothing coherent enough to convince Jolene that there wasn't a semiconscious six-foot-three man on her bathroom floor.

"I'm opening the door. I won't look." She opened it just enough so that her head fit, and she could hear him over the sound of the bathroom fan.

"I broke your towel rail. I'm sorry. I'll fix it," he sheepishly said.

Her eyes were shut, but the idea that behind her lids Jason stood possibly naked and definitely wet made her see stars.

"Oh, that's fine. Just place it against the wall or something. I'll call my landlord and he'll take care of it. That's if he picks up when I call. He doesn't, by the way. I haven't been able to use the light over the stove since—"

"Jolene," he interrupted her rambling.

God, she couldn't embody sexy mystique any less if she wore a shirt that listed her insecurities in alphabetical order.

"You can come in and open your eyes."

"Are you naked?"

"Yes."

Another wave of excitement washed over her. And when she opened her eyes and stepped fully into the bathroom, she found Jason holding her towel rail that he'd ripped from the wall. His wet hair swept across his forehead, and he looked a little bashful about the chaos he'd created. And oh yeah, he was also completely naked.

He'd shown up at Jolene's house without a previous plan, and he'd already broken her stuff, but it might've been worth it for the look in her eyes when she saw him naked. Her gaze made him hard, and sparks jumped across his skin as her eyes made their way up and down his body, lingering between his legs. He grew harder as the moments passed. It had required everything in him not to take Jolene against her printed couch the minute he saw in her natural element. But now, standing here, he wouldn't hold back.

"Come here," he rasped.

"But you're wet."

"You can dry me."

"But then I'll be wet."

He quirked his eyebrow at the double entendre, but her eyes sparked, and the tension and waiting culminated when she all but sprang into his arms. There was no timidity. Her lips grasped for his. They were full and plump and plied his open as he wrapped his arms around her body, feeling her curves under the light fabric of her T-shirt. He broke their kiss long enough to gauge her emotions. She looked hungry and ready for what their night would bring. He descended on her lips again, moaning at the familiarity of them. How sweet she tasted, how warm and utterly intoxicating her hands felt as they roamed his naked back and ass. He pushed her against the bathroom sink but felt no traction against the tile floor. He couldn't fuck her as hard as he wanted to against the sink.

"Bedroom?" His voice sounded rougher and louder than he intended.

She looked dazed up at him and grabbed him by his forearms and walked backwards into her room. She reached out for a kiss, and he held her back. If they continued at this pace, he would be coming before they had any real fun. He turned around and sat on the edge of her bed.

"Remove your clothes," he said.

She stopped before him and didn't hesitate before slowly removing her T-shirt. He groaned at the sight of her breasts clad in a lacy, turquoise bra, the color complementing her dark skin. She grabbed the heavy masses with her hands and squeezed them together. His dick jerked at the sight. Her hands moved away from her breasts and hooked at the waistline of her leggings.

"Slowly," he said.

Forcing himself to keep his hands at his sides, he watched as she revealed herself and stood in just her matching bra and panties. She then removed those, and her naked body was glorious. He took in her generous breasts and the way her waist narrowed slightly and flared out to hips and thighs that were made for the things he saw himself doing to her.

"Fuck." His resistance lapsed and he pulled her to him.

She stood between his legs, pressed up against him. He showered her chest with kisses while he played with her breast and palmed her ass. Jolene ran her hand through his still damp hair and traced his tattoo until all the senses he awakened made her lose her focus. One day she would finish outlining the tattoo with her fingers. He looked at her as if she was the most beautiful thing he'd ever seen, and she basked in the attention.

His head dipped and grabbed an already hard nipple he had been toying with into his mouth. He gently bit before sucking it. He made playful circles with his tongue then moved on to the other nipple, and he showed it equal enthusiastic attention. She was wet and had been since the moment she'd seen his amazing body. She touched herself, rubbing her clit and trying to find some relief. Jason lightly drew small circles with his fingers up her thighs, getting closer to where she needed him to touch her. He moved her hand and finally made contact with her pussy, and that brief contact made her head sling backwards. He teased her, not giving her the pressure or the full contact she desired.

"Oh, come on," she said.

He let go of her nipple and removed his hand. With agility and quickness that caught her off guard, he flung her onto her back on the bed. After drawing her body to the edge of the mattress and kneeling before her, he simply took her in. She felt his fingers on her and heard him moan.

"You're so unbelievably wet." He moved his finger down her slit, opening her up.

She could hardly breathe. He then lowered his head and placed his mouth onto her core. Her body writhed but he held her fast, keeping her legs apart. He lapped and circled her clit, and he fucked her with his fingers until she came.

He pushed her more squarely on the bed and kissed her soft belly and breasts before he kissed her mouth deeply. Jolene moved her hands, trying to find that impressive dick she'd seen. She whimpered when she finally found it, exploring and learning its contours, length, and girth. He pulled away.

"I need you," she said.

"Give me"—he kissed her neck—"one second." He got off of her and left the room.

When he returned, he held a box of condoms with one packet in between his lips. He placed the box on her bedside table. Jolene watched, enamored and delirious with lust as he rolled a condom over his dick.

He was once again on top of her. Caressing her hips and breasts and waist, pelting her with wet kisses, he leaned in toward her ear and whispered, "Tell me what you want."

She let out a frustrated groan. Why couldn't he just fuck her? "God, Jason. Please." She wiggled her lower half of her body and felt his dick press against her. Doing nothing but teasing her entrance.

"Tell me," he said, holding her still, but sounding more gruff and on edge than she'd ever heard him.

"I want your dick inside me, fucking me hard."

Without further delay, as if she had broken a spell with her words, Jason drove his cock into Jolene. She gasped at the sudden feeling of fullness and clutched at his broad, muscled shoulders. He withdrew himself and reentered with such force that she let out a shout at the subsequent sparks of pleasure that shot through her body. He did it again and again. Entering her and filling her, increasing his pace until she had to wrap her legs around his waist to remain anchored to him.

"Yes, wrap your legs tight around me," Jason said against her ear, smoothing her hair from her face. He braced himself on one arm then and placed his other hand between their bodies, finding and rubbing her sensitive nub. Driving her closer and closer to an orgasm.

"Oh, Jason, I'm coming."

"Come for me, Jojo," he urged.

And she did, hard and fast with his name on her tongue. She grasped at his back and hair as spasms coursed through her body. After several more hard thrusts, Jason also found his release with grunts and moans that came from the center of his chest. They lay there, with him partially on top of her, his weight a welcome presence as they came down from their euphoria. He rolled off of her after a while and disposed of his condom in the bathroom. But to Jolene's relief, he came back and tucked her against him.

"Incredible," he said. His voice sounded tired but content.

She giggled. "Yes."

Yes, you are.

Jason woke up in the middle of the night, a few hours before dawn, and needed water. The sex was spectacular. After fucking the first time, they'd slept for maybe an hour before going in for another round. Her soft, pliable body responding to his touch had filled a deep satisfaction in him. Just thinking about her moans and expressions of pleasure, stirred his dick again.

Thoroughly exhausted, Jolene slept next to him. He shifted and carefully unraveled himself from her body, making sure not to disturb her. He stood naked and watched her for a bit before heading over to her kitchen to find some water. After downing two full glasses he headed back to the warm bed and warmer body. He lowered himself and felt the bed dip under his weight.

"God!" Jolene jerked and shouted in fright.

"Hey, hey. It's just me." He gathered her in his arms. Pressing his lips to her forehead, he could feel her erratic pulse against his chest.

"I thought you left," she said as her dark silhouetted face turned up toward his.

"Nope, still here. Just grabbed some water. I can grab you some?"

"Yes, please."

He retraced his steps to the kitchen and retrieved a glass of water.

"I don't expect you to stay," she said as he placed the cool glass in her hand.

He instinctively and earnestly said, "I want to stay." He paused for a moment, a tension in his chest building. "As long as you want me to stay."

"Yes."

The tension evaporated.

"Then it's settled." He reentered the bed and slung his leg across Jolene's, placing the empty glass on the side table.

He drew her to him and breathed in the smell of her as she pressed her face into his hard chest. She melted against him, and he thought how right and comfortable this all felt. He definitely could get used to this.

Chapter 16

"So, he made you breakfast?" Yvonne asked as they stood near a craft service table. They were at a studio for a morning show their clients would appear on in the next hour. Jolene played with the pineapple chunk on her paper plate with a spoon, trying to make her recount as casual as possible.

"Yeah, he made us crepes. I don't have a crepe pan, but he made do."

"Hmmm."

Jolene turned to her friend who wore an ensemble that looked like something Stevie Nicks would've worn in the seventies—in the best way possible.

"What do you mean by 'hmmm'?"

"Absolutely nothing. I'm just proud and smug because a few weeks ago, you were swiping right on men whose personalities were Nietzsche quotes, and now you're getting good dick and crepes."

"You are so loud right now."

"I'm not."

"The words 'dick' and 'crepes' pretty much ricocheted off the ceiling, Yvonne. "

"Oh, please you're deflecting."

"I'm not deflecting anything. I just don't think people should know my business."

"Did I hear someone say crepes?"

Jolene gave Yvonne a pointed look. Mark, a host for the morning show, walked up to them. He'd obviously just strolled into the studio because he still held his bag and wore his designer sunglasses. He was a little taller than Jolene and, with his confidence and handsome face, he was regularly seen with beautiful women. His family came from the sort of money where if the world were to go up in flames, they had a literal spaceship to Mars ready to go.

He smiled up at Yvonne and wedged himself between the two women, essentially altering the dynamic he'd found. He was too slick. It was as if he had their conversation already plotted out, and he simply waited for her to say her lines so he could say his.

"Yes. I had crepes for breakfast this weekend. I haven't had them in a while."

"There's this creperie downtown that has eighteen different flavors." He shifted closer to Jolene. "We should go one of these days."

Jolene stepped closer to the wall on the other side of her. "Eighteen flavors. Wow. That's a lot. Isn't that a lot, Yvonne?"

"It sure is."

Yvonne's bored tone and blatant disinterest in their conversation made the interaction marginally entertaining. Mark, on the other hand, gave Jolene a crooked smile, as if he found her attempts to avoid a date with him amusing, adorable even. He'd asked her out when she met him at a media-networking event she'd attended when she first started working at Able & Quinn. They'd gone out to a fancy dinner, but Jolene had found the whole experience uninspiring. After the date, she'd gently let him know that it would be their last date. But ever since then, Mark had been a relentless flirt and on some mission to perhaps make her rethink her choice to never pick up what he put down. Mark had an appeal that Jolene recognized, but she found he didn't do anything for her, especially now.

Jolene indulged the man in conversation for a few minutes before she smiled at him. "We need to meet with our clients. I'll see you later, Mark."

The two women made their way to where their clients were getting their hair and makeup done to run through their talking points one last time.

"I'll just say this," Yvonne said, looking back at Mark —"it's rough out here. You deserve the fun you're having."

Jason worked on his second patient of the day, a man named Russell who loved to chat. He had to stop constantly to let the man get out what he wanted to say about his latest trip to Martha's Vineyard.

"Did you know that at one point people who lived on Martha's Vineyard used sign language as their main way of communicating? It didn't matter if they were deaf or not."

"That's fascinating. I didn't know that."

"It's—"

Jason cut Russell off with a gentle tap to the man's jaw, signaling he wanted him to open up. Marvin gave Jason a silent look of exasperation as he placed the suction against the inside of his patient's mouth.

The moment Jason removed his tools, Russell resumed

speaking. He pointed to the TV mounted on the wall. "My nephew's girlfriend works on that show."

Jason turned to the closed captioned TV and watched as a lively host interviewed two women. The names and their business scrolled at the bottom of the screen, and Jason recognized it as the business that his Jolene represented. He swiveled in his low chair, turning away from his patient to watch the women Jolene had prepped and coached to be the best they could be on TV. She probably watched them now off-screen.

"Doctor Akana?"

"Yes?"

"Everything good with my teeth?"

"Yes," Jason said as he turned away from the screen. He made a mental note to text Jolene about seeing her clients on TV. "Your gums are healthy and the swelling you were having issue with the last time has significantly improved. Marvin here will clean and floss your teeth, and you can be on your way."

"Thank you, Doctor."

"It's my pleasure, Russel."

After seeing his last patient that day, Jason changed into jeans and some sneakers he knew the kids at the after-school program he volunteered at would appreciate. Most people dreaded Mondays, but Jason liked them for the simple fact they were the days he volunteered.

When he arrived at the gymnasium, it was already packed with kids that reminded Jason of himself and the people he grew up around. He waved to one of the program facilitators, Tracey, before spotting some of the older kids, sophomores and juniors in high school, playing basketball.

"Hey, Jason!" shouted one of the boys, Anthony, who was tall and lanky. He waved from the sidelines, because despite his build, he wasn't as good as people assumed he would be so he was often benched. But the kid's talents were in other places. He loved science. Jason made his way over to Anthony, greeting the other kids he recognized along the way.

"Hey, man," Jason said, giving Anthony his fist to bump. "How's it going?"

"Good. Guess what?" Anthony reached under the bench he sat on for his backpack and retrieved a folded-up paper. "I got straight As on my final report card except for English."

Jason studied Anthony's report card. "That's what I'm talking about." He gave the young man a high-five.

He knew what it was like to have teachers, guidance counselors, and admission offices think you can't make it. He was so proud of Anthony. He'd been the poor, brown kid at college fairs and tours asking questions and trying to find and discover every scholarship and financial aid he was eligible for. Anthony would at least have some sort of guidance in the process.

"You just have to nail next year. But I would start applying for good scholarships now. You'll have a better chance of getting a full ride or at least a partial ride to a good school."

They watched the game unfold in front of them for a while.

"Your parents are doing well? Your siblings?"

"Yeah, Mom's got a new job. It's paying better but she's working longer hours."

Jason nodded. "And you start working again at McDonald's?"

"Yeah, next week." They remained silent for a while as they watched the game go into overtime. "Also, I kinda want to apply for a competition that the science center is holding." He said it so tentatively, like he was unsure that it was a good idea.

Jason forced himself to maintain a casual tone. No young person wanted to be fawned over. "I think that's a great idea. I'm down to help if I can."

Anthony nodded appreciatively.

The game in front of them ended and a new game was about to start. "Okay, enough of the serious stuff. Let's play some ball."

"Vacant building complexes?" Jason picked up the stack of real-estate ads on the edge of Jolene's coffee table. "Is this for your PR business?" He looked up at Jolene in her kitchen as she constructed a charcuterie board.

Her eyes went wide. "What?"

"You told me you're interested in opening up your own PR firm one day."

"You remembered that?"

He shrugged. "Yeah." Oh, he remembered a lot of things about Jolene.

She came over with the board and placed it on the table where the papers had been and let out a long sigh. "No. I was just looking." She took the papers from him and placed them on a shelf with an award he'd spotted when he first toured her place.

The abstract shaped trophy read, "2018 Young Professional of the Year." He wanted to give her encouragement and even opened his mouth to say something, but she beat him to it.

"And don't tell me to 'lean in' or some other platitude."

Jason kept quiet for a moment. "Well, since all I have are platitudes and I'm someone who knows almost nothing about public relations, all I'll say is that I've seen you in action and you seem like you know your stuff." He popped an olive into his mouth before feeding Jolene one. "Plus"— he lifted the award that sat on her shelf—"the people in your industry think so as well."

She smiled while she chewed. "Thank you. Now put it back and come eat the packaged food I artistically transferred to this board." She pulled him down with her as she sank into her couch.

They were making this arrangement work. Their hookups required they meet up right after work and at Jolene's apartment since it was close to both their respective workplaces. However, he didn't know what it meant when he constantly thought about taking her in his own bed. He didn't want to understand the psychology behind his desire to have her smell lingering on his sheets.

She turned the TV on to some reality show that had several middle-aged housewives screaming and throwing wine glasses at one another. She filled in the background information as they watched. Jolene's feet were in his lap, and he pointed at the TV trying to remember the characters' names she'd listed off.

"So, she's angry because the other woman wore the same dress to the reunion taping last season," he said.

"Yeah, pretty much."

He laughed at the theatrics of it all and found himself so transfixed with the drama unfolding that the low moan Jolene made took him a moment to recognize. He turned to her with his eyebrows raised.

She caught her bottom lip between her teeth and looked away. "Sorry." She pointed to where he idly massaged her feet. "I've been on my feet all day. It feels good."

He'd seen the heels she wore. Her collection littered

her entrance, and he thought about fucking her one day while she wore a pair. Possibly with one of those pencil skirts she wore to work hiked up around her waist. He gave her an impish smile. "I'm glad I can help."

"Oh, don't give me that look." She removed her legs from his lap. "I worked hard creating this board, and you'll eat it before you even think about anything else."

"I have to leave in an hour, and if we're friends-with-*benefits*, we ought to get to the benefits part," he said, shifting his suddenly tight pants while he crawled toward her end of the couch until he hovered over her.

She shrunk into the couch cushions, doing a poor job at containing a smile. "I think it's a benefit to be in my presence. Also, I'm quite content watching TV and receiving a foot massage."

"Liar. I bet you're wet as we speak."

"There's no way you can know that."

"So, you're telling me if I check, you won't be wet?"

"Yes."

He unbuttoned her jean shorts as he watched her closely. Her shallow breathing and the way her nipples pressed against the material of her shirt let him know that even if she weren't wet right now, it would be a quick fix.

He made contact with her damp panties. "As I said. Liar."

She shrugged. "What are you going to do about it?"

He tugged at her shorts until they were off her body and did the same with her panties. "Get on your hands and knees."

He saw the desire flare in her eyes and any sort of sass she might want to perform dissipated. She wore another one of her bralette-and-T-shirt combos, and when she turned around for her backside to face him, his breath caught at the tantalizing view. Grabbing a condom from his bag, he lowered his jeans and played with her pussy until her back arched and her breathing became labored. He rolled the condom over his cock and entered her with one fluid motion. She was so tight and warm. He grabbed her hips and gave her slow gentle strokes, encouraged by her soft whimpers. He reached under her and played with her clit as the tension in his own body built. He needed to go faster. Harder.

"Jason, faster."

He pressed his hand to her upper back so her face pressed into the sofa. Then he pumped assertively into her. She met his thrusts with her own movement, and the sounds their bodies made muddled with the TV's noise. She came, then, in a glorious expression of ecstasy. Her body squeezed his, and he was defenseless to his own orgasm. He withdrew from her and disposed of the condom before lying back on the couch with Jolene. He was there for he didn't know how long before he reached for his phone and saw the time.

"Shit." He sprung up. "I'm going to be late."

Jolene lazily rolled over and watched him as he got his belongs and bearings together. How had he lost track of time like this?

"You know, this wouldn't have happened if we just stuck to eating and foot massages."

He gave her an exasperated look before exiting her apartment. He shut the door behind him, leaving a laughing Jolene.

Jason was spared the third degree for exactly two weeks. He'd been late picking up his mother and aunt from the symphony where they'd listened to Hollywood hit songs throughout the ages. But he'd been surprised and relieved when he wasn't hounded about his whereabouts beyond a comment from his mother about him "never being late." He should've known that the women in his family didn't simply mute their opinions for too long. Jason couldn't do anything but smile listening to his aunt and mom on their podcast.

The sound of his aunt's voice filled his kitchen. "Unfortunately, we were unable to try drinks and hors d'oeuvres."

"Our driver, that is, my son arrived a bit late," his mom cut in. "We'd have driven ourselves or taken the bus if we'd known."

"But what we saw of the menu while the ushers whisked us to our seats looked good."

"But again, Jason—"

"Her son and my nephew."

"Yes. He seemed to lose track of time wherever he was beforehand, and we were late, so we can't tell you if the food was in fact good."

They knew he'd be listening, and it was their way of not only teasing him but also making sure tardiness wouldn't happen again. They went on to describe the performance, outline which songs the orchestra performed, and sprinkled in anecdotes about the earlier years of cinema. Leaning against his newly polished countertops, he texted their group chat.

Jason: I enjoyed the episode. :) Also, I was only 8 minutes late.

Mom: Remember we have another one coming up soon. It's the Dido and Aeneas opera.

He didn't have anything planned with Jolene, and he sort of hated that he didn't. Their hookups had begun to feel more than easy, breezy escapades. For instance, earlier that day she sent him a silly meme but also asked about how work went. He liked that there was someone who cared how the construction of the donair restaurant across the street drove him up the wall.

An incoming call from Ty interrupted his musings.

"How's the backyard renovation going?" Jason asked after initial inquiries about each other's well-being.

"Slow, but it's getting there. It has more space than it initially looked like. It's good because it's a lot of room to run and play." A long pause followed. "Which will be useful sooner than we expected."

"Are you guys getting a dog?"

Ty sighed. "No. I'm trying to tell you I'm going to be a dad."

Jason stood up straight. "Wow. Man. Congrats. That's amazing." He couldn't get the grin off his face. He'd known Ty when he first met Nicole, and he knew his friend was a goner the minute he saw him with his future wife.

"How's Nicole doing?"

"She's great. Sixteen weeks pregnant. I'm so excited, man."

"I'm so happy for you. Jolene must be pretty excited as well."

"Jolene? You guys still talk?"

Crap.

Jason tried to hold back on talking about Jolene. It would be awkward to discuss something that could be summarized with "it's just sex" with Ty because it was with his sister-in-law. And the guy was having a baby. This would sit low on his priority list, but he knew if he straight-up lied, Ty would know, and there would be more questions in the future.

"No, not really. We text now and again. Nothing serious. Just catching up and stuff."

And stuff? Jesus, it sounded like some awkward attempt

to hide the fact that he regularly had sex with his best friend's sister-in-law.

"Okay."

Shit.

His friend dropped the topic, but for the next fifteen minutes as they caught up, Jason couldn't help but feel like there, in fact, would be more questions in the future.

Chapter 17

"It looks like a blob," Yvonne said, studying the sonogram on Jolene's phone.

Jolene gave the image another look, moving her head side to side. "Well, kind of, but it's the first picture of my niece or nephew, so don't be alarmed if you find it framed on my desk."

Nicole's pregnancy was unexpected. The fact that she was pregnant so soon after landing a good job was less than ideal, but if anyone could juggle pregnancy, motherhood, and a busy work schedule it was Nicky.

"It would be the least weird thing that's shown up in our building," Yvonne said.

They looked at each other and laughed, simultaneously recalling how Jasmine from HR brought her iguana to the office for a few days while maintenance work was done in her home. Unfortunately, nobody knew about this temporary addition, and a few coworkers had found the reptile perched on the kitchen counter in the break room. Chaos ensued and panicked calls to animal control were made till Jasmine was able to explain the situation.

They were still laughing, and Jolene clutched at Yvonne's arm. "Stop making me laugh, my mascara is going to run. I can't look like a hot mess today."

Yvonne and Jolene made their way back from a quick coffee run to a big meeting with their boss and a few potential sponsors who came to talk about the logistics of Essential Essence Apothecary. Jolene needed to be alert and a bit bubblier than she usually was because at least one of the representatives responded well to dynamic presentations.

"Hey, you'll do fine," Yvonne said, noting her sudden nervous demeanor.

"God, I know. I just don't want to mess it up even a little bit."

They rode the elevator to their company's floor. When they stepped out, the usually sweet receptionist, Taylor, responded meekly to their greetings. Jolene should've known then that something was off, but if not with that, then perhaps she should've known when she noticed the lack of loitering interns.

"Is it me or is it very quiet in here?" Yvonne asked.

Jolene nodded as they turned a corner and found several of their colleagues, specifically the ones working on the Essential Essence Apothecary account, standing in front of their boss's closed office door. Fred, the graphic designer, had his ear pressed up against the door.

"What are you guys doing?" Jolene asked.

Three pairs of eyes turned to them, their faces grim and strained. Before Jolene could interrogate them further, the big door opened to reveal their boss, Craig Able. He looked displeased. His thick eyebrows pressed closely together as he studied them like he was some sort of Spanish bull and they a flailing red sheet.

"Everybody in," Mr. Able said.

All five of them quickly scurried into their boss's office and the spacious room with a large desk and generic paintings on the wall grew stuffy. The mechanical drone of the air conditioner did nothing but heighten the tension in the room. Craig Able was a short, solid-looking man who Jolene wouldn't be surprised to learn smoked expensive cigars and collected watches. He stood behind his desk, leaning heavily on his muscular arms.

"Where's Miss Baxter?"

Jolene raised her hand from her place against the door and squeezed past her coworkers to the front of the group.

"Tell me why I just got off the phone with Jessica Langley from Essential Essence Apothecary who informed me that she's firing us as her PR reps?"

Dizziness hit Jolene so fast and hard, it shocked her that she didn't find herself sprawled on the carpet.

"Wait, what do you mean?" Jolene asked, the words coming out in a rush.

Mr. Able set his eyes dead on her. "What words in that sentence didn't you understand?"

She shook her head and remained silent. What was going on? She had just spoken to Jessica and Carmen yesterday about this meeting, everything sounded good. Nobody was agitated. The backlash from the video had been taken care of. Sure, pasta emojis still appeared on their personal and business social media timelines, but it didn't overshadow the positive feedback and response their brand received.

"Does anyone have an explanation, since your leader seems to have lost her ability to speak?"

This couldn't be happening.

"Sir, I have no idea where this has come from. I just spoke with Jessica and Carmen yesterday, and they didn't express any misgivings, but I'll contact them right away and figure this out."

"Miss Baxter, this is the biggest contract you've ever led, and I thought you could handle it."

"I can, sir—"

"Evidently not, because you no longer have clients," he said. The room seemed to vibrate at the sound of his voice.

"I'll fix this." She would. If she had to literally beg Essential Essence Apothecary to take them back, she would do it. And if she had to be sweeter to Jessica and coddle the obviously egotistical woman, she would. Her eyes stung as tears threatened to spill, but she pressed her fingernails into the palm of her hand. She would not cry in front of this man.

"Make sure you do," Mr. Able said as he lowered himself into his chair. "Now, get out of my office."

As they left the room, Jolene felt the sympathetic glances of her colleagues. They knew how hard she'd been working to keep their testy clients happy.

Yvonne grabbed her hand. "Babe—"

"No, it's fine. I just need a moment. I'll email everyone with a plan once I figure one out," she managed to say.

Trying not to run or start wailing in the middle of the hallway, Jolene got to the restroom as fast as she could. Looking in the mirror above the sink, she expected tears to come but they didn't. Instead, she stared at herself for a long minute.

"You're going to fix this."

There wasn't any time to lick wounds or feel sorry for herself. She held her hands under cold water until she could no longer stand it. She dried them and put her now cold hands against her face and neck. Once in her office, she kicked off her heels and removed her blazer. She had work to do.

The July long weekend had snuck up on everyone. Jason had expected to spend it near a grill, but instead, he waited in line for drinks for his mom and aunt. They'd convinced him to extend his duties as an unpaid chauffeur and actually attend the opera with them. There was a backlog, and many of those who had ordered drinks were left to stand to the side and wait for their orders to be fulfilled.

"Popular show, isn't it?" asked a meticulously dressed man beside him.

Jason inwardly groaned. He didn't feel up to making small talk with a stranger at the moment, but he nodded and looked out at the foyer full of people waiting to be let into the auditorium.

"Personally, I'd rather be at a bar or something, but the things you do for women," the man said as he adjusted the cuffs on his expensive suit.

Jason nodded and gave a smile that he hoped didn't come off as a grimace.

"And, of course, she's being the social butterfly I love," he said, pointing to a group of people.

Already weary of the conversation, but determined not to be completely aloof, Jason cast a polite glance in the general direction the man pointed in. But Jason was taken aback when in his casual perusal of the foyer, he caught sight of Jolene standing with a group of women in their sixties and seventies.

He felt something leap in his chest. She wore a black cocktail dress with an asymmetrical neckline, and her curly hair was now straight and held in a high ponytail.

The man had not stopped talking, but it no longer grated on Jason's nerves. The stranger talked about the acoustics of the auditorium and how he ended up with some of the best seats in the place. Jason continued to watch Jolene, and when she looked up, they made direct eye contact. His pulse picked up in the base of his throat. He must've imagined the way her eyes lit up as she raised her hand to wave at him.

He and the man next to him waved simultaneously.

"You know Jojo?" the man asked.

Jason noticed that the man had stepped closer to him and watched as Jolene made her way toward them. Her dress hugged her hips and legs, making her strides shorter than usual. Immediately he envisioned himself peeling the dress off of her heated body and replacing it with his hands and tongue.

"Yes. Family friends," Jason responded.

Was this man Jolene's friend or work associate? Jason now really hoped that he hadn't come off cold.

"Ah, so you're probably familiar with how stubborn she is." The man nudged him on his arm with an elbow. "But it's just a matter of time."

Sure, Jason knew Jolene was willful, but it confused him why this man pointed this out to him, a virtual stranger. A nagging feeling at the back of Jason's neck ticked. "Sorry, just a matter of time?"

The man looked over to Jason. "Until Jojo admits she has feelings for me."

Jason's heart met his stomach at the base of his feet.

"She's playing hard to get," the man explained. "We once went to that French restaurant in the west side. I would highly recommend, by the way. We could barely keep our hands off each other long enough to eat our food. Thank God the car I used that night had roomy back seats."

The cocky smile on the man's face was the last straw.

"Excuse me," Jason said as he bypassed the man and

walked to the standing tables at the side of the foyer where his mother and aunt were waiting for the drinks he had abandoned.

"Jason, baby. What's wrong? Where are our drinks?" his mom asked.

His aunt touched his face with the back of her hand. "You look a little gray."

"It's nothing. Sorry. The line was extremely long." He grabbed his aunt's hand and squeezed it tenderly. "I'll take you guys somewhere after the show."

He tried to temper down the feeling of hurt that bubbled within him. He knew Jolene wouldn't break their agreement to exclusively sleep with one another until their arrangement was over, but he never thought she might currently be interested in someone else.

"That's okay." His mom shifted to see beyond his hulking torso. "Oh, Jolene."

The woman who was wreaking havoc on his internal equilibrium appeared next to him. She smelled of her trademark mango and coconut, and he clenched his jaw at the assault of the scent.

"Hi, Ms. Elizabeth." She gave his aunt a hug and did the same to his mom. "Hi, Ms. Nadine. How are you two?"

They engaged in small talk and his aunt and mom told her that this night out would be part of a future podcast episode. Jolene looked engaged and amiable as always, but she didn't acknowledge him at all.

"Where are your seats this evening?" Jolene asked.

His aunt showed her their tickets.

"I have really good seats, some of the best in the auditorium. I can trade with you. You two can sit in my and my friend Yvonne's seats."

"Oh, no, you deserve to experience what you paid for," his mom said.

"Don't worry. Yvonne's girlfriend is playing the part of Dido, so we got a discount on our tickets." Jolene was already taking the tickets from his aunt and placing the higher quality tickets in their stead. "Plus, we'll also be attending the show on closing night."

"Do you mind?" Aunt Liza asked him. He caught on then that she'd been watching him intently. He wasn't exactly exuding calm or any reasonable expression when it came to their current conversation. It was the question that finally drew Jolene's gaze up to his. She looked a little tired. Her eyes weren't as bright or expressive as they usually were. He squashed the impulse to draw her into his embrace.

"No, not at all," he said.

Jolene guided his mom and aunt in the right direction of their new auditorium entrance. He similarly walked toward his own entrance and mentally planned what he would say to Jolene when he called off their arrangement. He'd prefer to do it through text, but she deserved an in-person conversation. He'd have to check when he was available to meet her somewhere. Before he could make it to his auditorium door, Jolene intercepted his path and grabbed his forearm with a surprisingly firm grip and dragged him to the corridor of a nearby stairwell.

"Okay, whose pet did I kidnap?" she asked. She stood with her hands on her hips and her brows slightly furrowed.

Not one to mince words or play some coy game, Jason said, "Are you interested in dating someone else? Not that we're dating or that it really matters, but I don't want to be used to make someone you're actually interested in jealous."

Her back straightened and the furrow in her brow deepened. "What? Where is this coming from?"

Jason nodded toward where he and that man had been standing near the bar. "That man in the nice suit—"

"Mark?"

"Sure. He seems to be under the impression that you two are fated lovers or something."

She let out a choked sound. "He said that?"

"More or less."

"And you believed him?" She looked pissed now. "Oh my God."

"You haven't done anything wrong, I just—" What did he want? She wasn't dating Mark at the moment, but the idea that she simply bided time with him till she was ready to commit to Mark bothered him. A lot. He didn't know why, and he definitely couldn't tell her that. It sounded irrational and possessive.

She pinched the bridge of her nose. "He's someone I work with sometimes. I went out with him *once* when I first started working at Able & Quinn years ago. We didn't even kiss. I wasn't interested. But I didn't know he was going around claiming we're soul mates."

And just like that, Jason regretted everything. "Jolene, I'm sorry. It was none of my business, but I should've asked you about it instead of getting weird."

She stared at him for a long moment, and before the hardness in her face could soften, the buzz in the foyer got noticeably softer, indicating people were being let into the auditorium.

"We should take our seats," she said.

She didn't wait to see if he followed as she walked to their entrance. And because of the seat reshuffling several minutes earlier, he now sat beside Jolene and Yvonne. If the opera singers had done cartwheels across the stage, he wouldn't have noticed. He managed only to stew on the guilt he had for offending someone he really liked.

Jolene was stuck sitting next to Jason during her friend's opera. Her annoyance with Jason was nothing like the rage she felt for Mark, and from where she sat, she could see him sitting a few rows in front of her. She had the fleeting thought that she should've been more assertive when she rebuffed Mark's interest, but she dashed the idea away because she'd been clear. Mark had been the one who'd decided to ignore her signals. She felt hot with the mix of anger and embarrassment that surfaced when she thought about Mark misleading their mutual friends and acquaintances. How many people did she know who believed her and Mark were in some type of relationship?

Instead of concentrating on the way Yvonne's girlfriend, Diana, perfectly played the soprano part of Dido, she fumed. When it wasn't about Mark, it was about how disappointed she was with Jason for doubting her. For making her feel horrible even if it were momentary. Because when she'd spotted him across the foyer, she nearly sank into the floor when she recognized the look he gave her. It was the same one he'd given her throughout the years, full of coldness and distance. She hadn't appreciated till then how she'd become accustomed to the playful glint in his eye that let her know he was ready to verbally spar with her.

The last few weeks she'd been feeling frazzled, having to deal with her work setback, and she thought she at least had one aspect of her life in order. This fight, unlike the numerous squabbles they'd had before, felt more personal and real. She and Jason would most likely discuss this in some long, drawn-out conversation. She hated big, serious discussions about states of relationships. She had dozens of them throughout her short-lived marriage. They were just emotional excavations that left her feeling nauseous and even more confused with the status of the relationship.

For now, she had to tolerate sitting next to him for the next two hours. His body, too big for the smallish theatre seats, brushed up against her. If her dress weren't so restrictive, she might've crossed her legs or leaned into the side where Yvonne sat.

Diana ended the aria she sang, and Jolene clapped diligently; however, she had a pang of guilt over not giving her friend's performance her undivided attention. But after a tense intermission and more impressive singing, the opera ended and Jolene was ready to hightail it out of there before she had to interact with Jason further.

However, she had to say goodnight to Ms. Elizabeth and Ms. Nadine, and she also had to wait for Yvonne and Diana who she was giving a ride home. So, they all stood in a circle in the entranceway that other opera attendees vacated.

"That was fantastic, wasn't it, Elizabeth?" Ms. Nadine asked.

Ms. Elizabeth nodded, pressing her hands to her chest. "Exquisite."

They gushed over particular performers and were delighted to meet Diana when she finally emerged from backstage. The petite opera singer with dark, lush, wavy hair and arresting eyes met her girlfriend with a kiss and took the praise with grace.

"Di, this is Elizabeth and Nadine. They're"—she briefly looked at Jason—"family friends."

"We would love if you would join us on an episode of our podcast," Ms. Nadine said almost immediately.

"I would enjoy that. It would have to wait till the season is done, though."

During this exchange, Jolene and Jason stood awkwardly apart, listening and nodding and smiling where appropriate. She caught Yvonne's eye and with telepathy that had been built and fortified through years of friendship, Jolene sent out an SOS signal.

"It's getting late, we should really be heading out," Yvonne said soon after.

"Oh, yes." Ms. Nadine looked at her smartwatch. "It is." They all said their farewells, and Jolene briefly made eye contact with Jason. He looked as if he wanted to say something to her and he actually might have, if she hadn't averted her eyes. The family finally disappeared from their view.

Jolene hugged Diana. "You're the best Dido I've ever seen."

"This is literally your first time seeing the opera," Diana said as she returned the hug and laughed.

"An irrelevant technicality."

"I'm just going to use the restroom before we go," Diana said.

Yvonne had been studying Jolene and finally asked, "Girl, what's going on?"

Suddenly feeling drained from the things falling apart in her life, Jolene closed her eyes. "I don't want to get into it tonight."

"Fine. Just don't bottle it up too long, okay?"

Jolene nodded and gave her friend a reassuring smile. She would tackle this problem later. For now, she wanted to wallow in misery.

Chapter 18

JASON HAD BEEN RUNNING a lot in the past week. The problem with that was he wasn't a runner, at least not a long-distance runner. Give him a football or a Frisbee and he could make it down a field, otherwise it was a no-go. He kept his fitness up by lifting weights and running sprints on the treadmill. But he'd chosen to forsake his God-given sense and pick up the habit because it was the only way he found he could sleep through the night. Without it, he'd wake up hours before his alarm was set to go off to rub one out because of a vivid sex dream he had about Jolene.

He lived in hell wanting someone so much but having to fight the impulse to contact her. There'd been several times he'd been a click away from ordering a bouquet of gardenias to Jolene's office. He stopped short every time only because it struck him how presumptuous it was. He'd already apologized the night of the opera, and her silence was answer enough. He had to respect and accept that. But that left him biding his time until that weird longing for Jolene's company went away.

It was only now that Jason fully grasped how his

hookups with Jolene had disrupted his schedule. He no longer needed to reshuffle workouts and spending time with his family to find time to hang out with Jolene. That should've made settling back into his long-standing routine easier, but dissatisfaction nagged at him more than it had when he realized his life was stagnant. He'd finally left his comfort zone and discovered that he liked being there.

To battle this new restlessness, he'd tried eating dinner in the park across the street from his apartment instead of in front of the television. But it only helped the first time he tried it. The search to find respite in what had become a too-restrictive routine was why he currently sat in a bar with the staff from the clinic for happy hour. The fact he rarely socialized with them was clear because he failed to find any of the jokes and stories they told funny. He stirred the ice cubes in his glass with his straw and tried to pick up the song that played over the chatter in the bar.

Janet, a dental hygienist, noticed that Jason was out of the loop. "Dr. Akana, I can't believe you actually came out with us."

The party of eight turned to him as if just realizing that it hadn't been a hallucination when he accepted their invitation for drinks and appetizers. Jason took a sip of his water and smiled, not really knowing how to respond to the obvious assertion that he was somewhat of a loner.

"He's probably sick of us always asking and decided to just throw us a bone and grace us with his presence," Malcolm, a fellow dentist said.

Jason laughed with everyone else. "Trust me, you're the only one besides maybe my mother who wants to be around me right now."

Jolene walked into the meeting with Carmen and Jessica determined not to look defeated. She'd worn her best suit and a pair of heels that made her stand taller than some men in the office. With her, she brought a single piece of paper that outlined additional services she suspected the apothecary owners were looking for.

"All right, let's hear it," Jessica said once they were all seated in a boardroom at Able & Quinn.

Jolene looked between the two women. Carmen maintained a blank expression, probably trying to avoid undermining the negotiations with her usual sympathetic glances. Jessica, well, she was doing her best impression of an intimidating Robert De Niro character.

"First, I'd like to hear from you why you fired us," Jolene said, placing her hands on the desk.

Jessica leaned back into the seat and crossed her arms. "I didn't think you were serious about our campaign."

Jolene clenched her teeth and took a moment before saying, "How so?"

"I wasn't seeing results."

There was evidence Jolene could provide that showed the effectiveness of her work, but statistics and numbers were not going to win her back this account. "You're building a brand. Recognition won't happen overnight unless you know Oprah or you *are* Oprah. But despite that, I've done a good job boosting your visibility."

Carmen shifted in her seat.

Jolene needed them to see they'd be lost without her. She was the life buoy they were inconveniently leaving behind to venture into unknown waters. "You're supposed to launch in seven weeks, who do you think knows your company and customers enough to pull it off?"

Carmen sat up straight and said, "We do."

The tension in Jolene's jaw was building. She'd debated

what tactic to use during this meeting, and she realized that Carmen might respond to a more gentle approach but Jessica wouldn't. And they all knew who was running the show.

"Are you willing to take that gamble?" Jolene asked. "You are experts on the products you sell, but are you confident enough in your ability to convince other people to care about your brand and company?" She let the silence hang for a beat. "Because I am."

Carmen nervously looked at her partner. Jessica had taken to tapping a furious rhythm on the table with her fingers.

Jolene let them sit with their thoughts, hoping doubt swirled within them.

"I need people to stop hating me," Jessica finally said.

Jolene let out a breath. It was as she thought. Jessica's ego was taking a beating from all the social media backlash, and she was disappointed that Jolene hadn't made it disappear.

Jolene slid the paper she'd brought with her in front of the women. "We can work on that."

Later that day, Jolene found herself in another difficult spot trying to keep her butt in the air in a downward dog position. Yvonne effortlessly maintained the pose with her lithe frame.

"And we're going to stay here for a while. Peddle your legs and feel the muscles in your calves stretch. Go back to your intention whenever you feel like you're collapsing," the yoga instructor said from her place at the front of the room.

Jolene had succeeded in regaining Essential Essence

Apothecary as clients. There would be more TV and radio appearances to further counter the public's perception of Jessica. Jolene had been able to book a last-minute segment on the morning news for a few days from now that would highlight the rise of local women-owned businesses.

"I'm trying to see how I can spend the least amount of time with Jessica and Carmen," Jolene said. She kept her voice low and peeked under her armpit to look at Yvonne.

They moved into some position called warrior pose that made Jolene's legs wobble. Yvonne opened one eye and looked at her. "Are you sure you don't want me to go instead?"

"Yes, I'm sure—"

There was a shushing sound from someone upfront.

Jolene lowered her voice even more. "It's a simple TV interview. I might have to get lunch with them, but I'll be back in the office early afternoon."

"You have an entire team behind you if something comes up. Remember that."

They transitioned into cobra pose.

"And if you just want to vent and bitch. Call me," Yvonne said.

Jolene hoisted herself the best she could into a downward dog once again, feeling appreciative of Yvonne's support over the past two weeks. In fact, all her colleagues had been great. It was the type of professional but kind work environment she wished existed throughout the company. If she ever got her dream PR firm started, that would be something she would work to foster.

The chaos at work had left her too emotionally drained to think about Jason and how awkward they'd left things. Whatever they had going on prior to the night of the opera no longer existed. That should've been fine; Jolene's arrangement with Jason was supposed to be casual and temporary anyway. But despite her best intentions, their interactions hadn't felt like an appendage to her regular life. They'd felt weirdly intertwined and important. So, here she was, in a lopsided tree pose, wishing she'd called him a few days after the opera.

"Thank you, girl," Jolene said her voice catching a bit.

Yvonne looked over, squinting in the low-lit studio. "You better not be crying during yoga. If you start, I'll start."

"I'm a cold-hearted zombie. I don't cry."

Yvonne snorted a little too loudly, receiving another hush from somewhere in the room. "That's what you want the world to think."

Anthony stood in front of Jason and a few of the other community center kids who had been willing to sit and give Anthony feedback on his presentation for the science competition. He ran through his hypothesis and evidence; it was clear and persuasive. Jason nodded throughout the monologue, following along, and trying to access the dormant knowledge on introductory chemistry. He clapped once Anthony bowed.

"Yeah, I don't know what the hell you said, but you sounded smart as shit," said a boy around twelve years old named Christopher who hadn't looked up from his phone the entire time Anthony presented.

"I think you'll win," said Trisha, a fourteen-year-old with braids and braces.

"Good job, Anthony," the program coordinator said from her place where she monitored the rest of the kids running around the gymnasium.

Anthony looked expectantly at Jason, waiting for his critique.

"You have an interesting experiment with a competent hypothesis. Your evidence and explanation of it were thorough. It's really good. But I think your presentation could be improved."

The young man shuffled where he stood and waited for Jason to expand on his point. If Jason had learned anything about PR from spending time with Jolene, it was that presentation and how you're perceived could do a lot of the legwork in convincing an audience to invest or take interest in your brand, or in Anthony's case, his argument.

Jason left the wooden bench he sat on with the rest of the kids. He moved toward Anthony's neat, but simple poster paper. "You could use more colors for the different sections. It'll help you stand out in a sea of black-and-white font at the competition."

Anthony nodded, understanding.

"Also, when you present and recite your information try to pause and look up once in a while. Nobody wants to stare at the top of your head."

"I get nervous, man."

"Practice your speech till you don't even have to think about what you're saying anymore. It'll help."

"My teacher told me to look at the audience's foreheads instead of in their eyes," a girl named Danielle offered.

Jason pointed to Danielle. "That's a good tip. Also, you can hold the Wonder Woman pose for a few minutes"—Jason demonstrated by putting his hands on his hips and throwing his shoulders back—"before getting in front of the judges. Studies show that it'll make you feel more confident."

Anthony looked skeptically at Jason. "I don't know,

man, sounds like some fluff psychology."

Jason raised his hands. "Listen, you've got nothing to lose by trying it out."

Anthony let out an exhausted breath. Jason was tempted to emphatically declare that he'd win, but he knew he couldn't make that assertion.

"Can we leave now?" Christopher asked, directing the question at Anthony.

Anthony shrugged and the bench cleared.

"All you can do is be well prepped and put your best foot out there," Jason said. He encouragingly patted Anthony on the back. "And lucky for you I'm a perfection-ist, so I have a few more things you can improve upon."

Anthony gave him a nod and a smile. "Okay, I'm listening."

Later that evening, Jason arrived home from his evening run. His shirt was soaked and his heartbeat still erratic, but the session had been the fastest he'd run since he started his bizarre "get over Jolene" regimen. It had been a long day. In addition to volunteering, he'd also performed wisdom teeth extractions on two different patients. He enjoyed the process. It was a little bit of an art. But he'd made the mistake of once mentioning that to a patient when he first started practicing. It didn't really comfort people to know their dentist enjoyed a process that would probably cause them discomfort for several weeks to come.

He was slowly getting back into the groove of every-thing. And he'd finally succumbed to Mrs. Bayuk's suggestions he go out with her granddaughter, and they had a date scheduled for tomorrow. He removed his head-phones from his ears and let his music fill his kitchen as he chugged his protein shake and stretched his hamstrings and quads. The EDM music he preferred to run to was suddenly replaced with the ring of an incoming call. Without looking at the caller ID, he picked up the phone. His mother was the only one who'd call him at this time.

"Hellooo," he said, drawing out the word in the way his mom usually answered her own calls.

"Hi, Jason?"

Jolene.

Her voice, the way she said his name. It was like he'd been wandering a desert and had just gotten his first sip of water. He savored the sound for a moment, but failed to find his voice, his brain trying different conclusions on for size instead. Had she forgiven him? Was she still annoyed?

Dammit.

"I'm sorry to bother you. And I know we left on bad terms. I wouldn't be calling if it weren't important. And I'll completely understand if you don't want to talk to me right now—"

"Jolene, what is it?" His heartbeat refused to slow down.

"I need the biggest favor, and I don't know if it's something you're even allowed to do." She took an audible breath in. "I have clients. They're supposed to appear on live TV tomorrow, but they mixed up the radio and TV interview dates. And that wouldn't be a big deal except"—she took another breath—"one of them planned to get her teeth whitened before the TV interview because she couldn't stand how they looked the first time she appeared on TV."

She spoke so fast. He could hear how anxious she was, and he had the intense desire to see her and soothe her.

"She's threatening to not show up. Which would mess up everything. And so this is where I ask you: Can you do an emergency teeth whitening? I know it's technically not a dental emergency, but it's a career emergency."

He let her words settle in him. Processing everything she said. And even before he articulated anything, he knew he would help her.

"What time is the interview tomorrow?"

"Eleven o'clock."

"My first patient arrives at eight o'clock," he said, mentally seeing what he needed to do to make this work. "Your client will have to come in before we're officially open at 6:30 a.m. It will take ninety minutes to complete the procedure, and by the time it's complete, the receptionists will have started for the day and can go through billing everything."

"Thank you, Jason." There was emotion in her voice she failed to hide.

Jason grabbed the back of the chair in his kitchen. "You'll be there too, I'm assuming?"

"Yes. I'll be there as well."

His heart soared, and he took several seconds to compose himself. He didn't want to make her wary of seeing him again. They said goodbye, and Jason called the owner of the clinic and let him know he would be doing a teeth-whitening treatment before the clinic opened. Then he made an alert on his phone to pick up donuts for the receptionists.

He settled into bed after taking a shower and eating a dinner he didn't really taste. He had worked out and had a busy day at the clinic and that would usually grant him a dreamless night. But he did dream that night. Nothing sexy, but it was as if his brain had finally been given permission to once again think of the beautiful woman with a smile and spunk that could light up a room. His Jolene dry spell was almost over.

Chapter 19

JOLENE SAT in the parking lot of Nottingham Dental, anxious and wary. She looked at her image in the front viewing camera of her phone for the third time, making sure she looked all right. She glanced at the car parked beside her. Jessica and Carmen sat there waiting for the dentist she had dismissed quite strictly a fortnight ago. They were the only cars in the complex that held Jason's dental office, a coffee shop, a gas station, and a small grocery store.

She had almost gone off on Jessica for her stubbornness about her teeth having to be whitened. She had pushed and pleaded with Jessica to reconsider, but the woman had felt some type of way at the few comments that had mentioned her teeth on her last TV appearance and wouldn't budge. She even pulled the "I can call Mr. Able and see what he has to say about this" card, and Jolene had racked her brain for solutions. She had thought about whitening strips and toothpaste you get at the drugstore, but Jessica insisted they weren't strong enough.

Then the solution appeared in her head like a gopher

popping out of a hole in the ground. The dread of having to explain everything overshadowed the thrill of relief that passed through her. How would she ask for a favor from someone she hadn't accepted an apology from? She'd half expected Jason to hang up on her or at least scoff at her attempt. But he hadn't. He hadn't even sounded amused or self-satisfied at her groveling. He had simply offered a solution. She pressed her head into the steering wheel, willing for the day to go at turbo speed. The dry bagel and orange juice she had for breakfast had settled weirdly in her stomach.

A soft tap interrupted her thoughts. She jolted and looked out. And there he was, her knight in blue scrubs at six a.m. She'd never seen him in his work garb. It was appealing and sexy. Like he could be part of one of those medical dramas where everyone is hot and sleeps with one another. He stepped back, allowing her to exit her vehicle.

"Hi."

"Hey."

Jessica and Carmen left their own vehicle. A hushed but tense conversation between the two women unfolded.

"Thank you again for doing this," Jolene said.

"Don't mention it."

It was a flippant response some people used as an alternative to "you're welcome," but the way he said it, it was as if he desperately wanted her to view this not as a favor but as a mea culpa.

Jolene didn't know how long they stood there looking at each other, the electricity jumping and sparking between them. They probably looked like two glaciers daring the other to melt. If it hadn't been for the rude grunt that came from Jessica, Jolene wasn't sure they would have moved.

"Dr. Akana, this is Jessica. You'll be working on her today. And this is her business partner, Carmen."

The three of them exchanged handshakes, and Jessica gave Jason a scrutinizing once-over.

"Nice to meet the both of you," Jason said as he guided all three women toward the entrance of the clinic. He turned off the security alarm and motioned to the waiting room seats. "Once I finish preparing my station, I'll come get you, Jessica. The procedure will take ninety minutes, then you can be on your way."

Jason looked at Jolene, then, and the final bits of anger and frustration she'd held onto in an attempt to keep regret at bay, vanished.

———————

Jason had cancelled his date with Mrs. Bayuk's grand-daughter Bailey. He felt kind of guilty. But after seeing Jolene this morning, he didn't know if he could be present or not compare Bailey to Jolene. That fact alone bothered him because Jolene and he weren't dating. They weren't even doing their "just sex" thing anymore. He placed his keys on the hook near the door and slung his work back-pack behind his kitchen chair. The current heavy, summer rains raging outside his window would prevent him from going on his run.

His cancelled date and the downpour would also keep him near his phone where he hoped Jolene would at least text him. She had left early in the morning after he'd brightened Jessica's teeth. The woman had been a prickly patient. But her attitude had been mild compared to what he'd dealt with over the years. As long as he kept his tone even and his responses succinct, difficult patients had nothing to latch on to and usually became a little less irritable.

His phone rang and he looked at the caller ID to prevent yesterday's gaffe, then he tempered down his glee when he saw it was Jolene. He hadn't summoned her like a genie in a bottle; she was probably just calling to thank him again. Even though she had done enough of that through text message.

"How did the TV appearance go?"

"It went smoothly. No more hiccups." There was silence, then. "But I want to thank you again for everything you did today...I'm currently in the parking lot of an Indian restaurant with enough rice, butter chicken, naan, and tikka masala to put two grown adults into a food coma. Do you want to share?"

It would the best unexpected development to his schedule that day. "Yes."

Jason's place didn't look exactly what she'd thought it would look like. It was obviously very neat and organized. The umbrella he'd met her with in the parking lot had a cradle it belonged in and so did his house keys, mail, and shoes. But his place was also warm and full of life and his quirks.

"Number one son, eh?" she asked, holding up the bright blue and yellow mug with the bubble letter text.

"Would you believe me if I told you I bought it for myself?"

"Yes, because you're an arrogant bastard."

He smirked and took a sip from his own mug decorated with some comic book superhero Jolene knew she should've known the name of. Jason had handed her a cup of tea once he'd set their dinner on the kitchen counter. He gave her a quick tour of his apartment. She tried not to show too much interest in his bedroom, and she immediately chased away the thought about how nice it would be to bury her face in Jason's sheets. She took note of his 1950s German radio record player.

"It was my dad's," he said.

She ran a finger across the low, vintage sound box, wanting to ask more questions about his dad, but settled on saying, "It's really beautiful."

They got comfortable at his small kitchen table, digging into the food she had brought.

She knew they should discuss their argument and misunderstanding the night of the opera, but she liked the easy, breezy conversation they were having over bomb-ass food.

Later.

"You have a large collection of pots and pans." She looked at the dozen stainless steel equipment that hung on a metal pot rack.

"Some of them I've had since my college years."

A man liking and knowing how to cook shouldn't impress her so much. She could've sworn her bar sat a little higher than that, but here she was impressed. "So, you weren't the ramen-eating college student?" She took a bite of her naan. "Must've been nice."

He laughed a little. "No, I was definitely too poor and didn't have a safety net to eat anything really fancy in college. But previous students left that pot"—he pointed to a small pot that looked out of place next to the newer more shiny pans—"in my freshman dorm room. I've had it ever since."

They finished their meals in companionable silence, listening to the heavy rains hitting the windows. Once they were done, they cleared their plates, and she stood beside him holding a dishcloth as he scrubbed their dishes clean.

"I'm sorry I hurt you," he said.

No time like the present to broach uncomfortable conversations. "At first, I was annoyed that you believed Fuck Face Mark's lies, but I can't fault you too much because I probably would've too. So, no apologies needed." She smiled at Jason, then. "Thanks for answering the phone when I needed you, though."

He let out an audible exhale and returned the smile. "Would it screw up the moment to know that I didn't see the caller ID before answering?"

Jolene laughed, and Jason handed her a newly cleaned plate to dry. They let the remaining tension fizzle away, and she felt lighter and grateful that she hadn't lost his friendship.

"'Fuck Face Mark' is a lovely name, by the way," he said.

"I tried to find words to make it a three-word alliteration, but Yvonne convinced me 'Fuck Face Mark' was just fine."

Suddenly a heavy flash of lightning brightened the window, and loud, obnoxious thunder followed several seconds after.

"You should probably wait out this storm," he said, turning the running water off.

She looked outside the window. "You're probably right."

"You can even stay here overnight, if you want."

She felt her body shiver like one of those lightning bolts connected with her core. Mother Nature: her wing woman.

"Is this your not-so-subtle way of getting back to our

fuck buddy status?" She emphasized the words, knowing he hated it.

He dramatically shuddered, letting her know he knew what she had just done. But he didn't respond beyond a small smile. While he continued to wipe down the area around the sink, Jolene took a step away from the counter and attempted to land the sponge in the caddy attached to the sink like she was making a free throw on a basketball court. She missed the intended mark. Jason retrieved the sponge and similarly tried to throw it into the caddy. He missed as well. They turned to one another with smiles and a lighthearted game followed. After several more attempts, Jolene proved victorious.

She raised two fists in the air. "I knew my beer pong skills would be useful one day." She'd missed their silly competitiveness, and her body relaxed with the familiarity of it.

"And what will you take as your prize?" he asked as he inched closer to her.

She looked around his small kitchen, ignoring how dark his eyes had turned. "What do you have to offer?"

"You can take whatever you like." The muscle in his strong jaw ticked. "But I'm not going to lie, all I can think about right now is how much I've missed your body and fucking you."

Such simple words, and yet she felt a pulsing between her legs and saw stars like he'd just quoted some renowned poet. Her body moved toward his on its own volition, and she grabbed him by the T-shirt and brought his mouth to hers, warmth emanated from them both. Their tongues danced, and she bit his lip. He returned the favor, and she felt him wrap his arms around her middle and knead the flesh he found there. Drawing her flush to his body, her nipples hardened against him. She needed to get out of her clothes.

Another lightning-and-thunder combo interrupted their make out in front of the sink, but Jason used it as an opportunity to hoist her off the kitchen's tile floor. She gasped at the sudden levitation. She wasn't a small or a necessarily short woman.

"Oh my God, put me down."

"No. Wrap your legs around me."

She planned on protesting, but she recognized the stubborn glint in his eye. He would just stand there holding her until she did so. She wrapped her legs around his torso, and he shifted to readjust her position. All she could think about while he walked them toward his bedroom was what she would tell the 911 operator when his back gave out. But her anxiety amounted to nothing because they arrived at his bed without any catastrophic incident, and Jason dumped her onto it and resumed giving her long and brain-muddling kisses.

They found their way out of their clothes, and the thunder couldn't stop them once they were delirious with need. Jolene lightly bit and licked Jason's shoulders and neck as he played with her clit with his thumb. She threw her head back, oscillating between moaning his name and saying "yes."

"You look stunning when you're turned on," he whispered. He kissed the side of her mouth before quickly retrieving a condom.

He placed the condom on himself before settling on his back. Without prompt, Jolene straddled his hips, and before he could appreciate the view of her on top of him, she pressed herself down onto his cock. She stayed still for a few beats, adjusting to the new position. Refusing to do what his body wanted him to do, he took calming breaths. He wanted to roughly and aggressively pull her up and bring her back down to his cock's hilt, but he'd let her set the pace. Before long, she moved up and down his length at an intoxicating rhythm. She whimpered and moaned, and suddenly, as if a switch went off, she planted her hands on his chest and looked him dead in his eyes and sped up her movements.

However, it wasn't fast enough. Not hard enough. Jason grasped her hips and pitched his own hips up, forcing her to abandon her rhythm and just hold on as he planted his feet into the mattress and thrust up into her pussy. God, he'd missed the feeling of her. He was so close, but he couldn't let himself come till she had her release. He put his thumb in his mouth then reached for her clit, pressing and rubbing it until her mouth opened on a silent scream, and he felt her clench around him.

"That's it, baby," he said.

Her body convulsed on top of him. At that point she collapsed onto his chest, and he moved to wrap his arms around her waist. Her breath tickled the side of his face as he took several more pumps and reached his peak.

"Jolene!"

He continued to say her name. In whispered, barely there sounds against her throat. He was content to keep her on top of him, her weight a reassurance that she was still with him. With the sound of the rain slowing its torrent path, she fell asleep against him, and he knew that there wasn't any other place he'd rather be.

Chapter 20

"DID you get the email I sent you about the food vendors for the launch?" Yvonne asked the second she entered Jolene's office.

Jolene looked up from her screen where she'd been focused on some detailed work. She stared at Yvonne for a moment and mentally ran through the number of emails she had lying in her inbox, trying to recall which one she referred to.

"The Italian food vendor," Yvonne prompted.

"Yes. I'll email them about what promotional things they can bring."

Yvonne had flippantly suggested that the Italian restaurant from Jessica's scandal should cater Essential Essence's launch party, and Jolene had seized on the idea. They would be able to mend a relationship between two local businesses and continue to improve the public outlook on Jessica.

Yvonne pursed her lips.

"I know. I know. Jessica is going to flip, but I'll talk to her first. Don't let her get wind of it till then."

"All right, boss."

Jolene stood and stacked her binders and folders into her gigantic bag. "I want you to know I love you for calling me boss."

"I know. That's why I do it."

Yvonne moved out of Jolene's way as she grabbed a file on a shelf behind her.

"Where are you going? Don't tell me Jolene Baxter is leaving the office before six."

Jolene fluffed her hair a bit. "I've got a hair appointment."

"Wow. I'm shocked."

"You're making it seem as if I neglect myself and walk around with limp curls and dull hair."

"No. You always look great. It's just knowing you as I do, you would have cancelled it to spend one more hour at the office."

Jolene shrugged. She had been feeling really content with where she was in life and things were going great. Why not pamper herself?

"It's good. You deserve good things, that's all."

Jolene mouthed *thank you* to her friend as they made their way to the elevator.

"Oh, I literally cackled listening to Di's podcast debut. Jason's mom and aunt are adorable."

"They've already recorded and posted?" Jolene pressed the elevator button.

"Sure did."

"I'll listen to it on my commute."

The elevator door opened.

"Remember to send me pictures of your hair."

"Always."

The elevator doors closed between the friends, and Jolene pulled out her phone as she descended.

Jolene: The article I was talking about last night.

She included a link to the piece in a following text.

Jason: I'm at the gym. You just interrupted my music.

Jolene smiled. Someone was feeling sassy. She sent him an eye roll emoji.

Jolene: You could've ignored me then. No need to respond.

Jason: Ha!

Jason: I'll read it when I get home, thank you ❤

Jolene stared at the heart emoji for a bit too long and felt her own heart stop and start at its presence. It was just a casual way to end of a sentence. She littered her own texts with them when she texted her family and friends. No need to over analyze. Preoccupied with trying to decide whether to respond to Jason's text, Jolene barely registered that someone had entered the elevator with her.

"Hey, Jolene."

She tensed and looked up at the man she'd been avoiding.

"Hello, Mark."

"You haven't been returning my emails."

She looked straight at the elevator buttons and slipped her phone back into her purse. She could feel him leisurely leaning against the side of the back wall of the elevator looking at her.

"I'm positive that one of my colleagues has responded to all your requests and questions," she said. She'd debated for days on how to rebuke and interrogate Mark about his blatant lies about the nature of their relationship, but each scenario ended with him making their working relationship miserable. She didn't know if it was worth it to make things awkward when so much of the success in her career so far was because of the access she had to different media outlets.

"You seem pissed."

She spared him a glance and feigned obliviousness. "Nope."

"All right, in that case do you want to grab drinks tonight?"

"No, I have somewhere to be."

"What about sometime when you don't?"

The anger she tried to contain for the sake of cordiality surged to the surface, and she turned to him, clutching her purse in front of her. "Why? So, you can legitimize the lie about us dating?"

He had the gall to look amused. "Are you actually angry that I want to take you out?"

The elevator door opened to the ground level and she walked out. Mark did too.

"That's a compliment where I'm from."

"There's no relationship, and it's rude and unprofessional of you to insinuate that to anyone," Jolene hissed, taking care not to draw attention from the security at the front desk and the lingering people in the foyer.

"Jojo—"

She hated the way he used her nickname.

"We've been doing this flirty game for years. I thought that you'd appreciate the bold move," he said.

God. The man had taken niceties and tolerance and spun it into something it clearly wasn't.

"Let me be clear here and now. I am not interested in any sort of relationship with you apart from the professional one we share." She gave him a curt nod and didn't wait for him to respond. She could feel the pressure building up in the base of her neck with every step she took. She felt lightheaded, but she continued until she got into the safe confines of her car.

She had the impulse to cancel her appointment, but she forced herself, with shaky hands, to pull up Ms. Elizabeth and Ms. Nadine's podcast and let their intro music and fast chatter drown out any anxiety she felt.

Yvonne was right, she deserved to treat herself, and Mark wasn't going to screw that up for her today.

"That's a new one?" Jason asked as he pointed to a dress that hung on the edge of Jolene's wardrobe.

They'd just spent the better part of the afternoon giving one another orgasms. She inwardly smiled at the memory of her going down on him. Just thinking about wrapping her mouth around his dick got her wet, and the way he had fisted her hair and made noises that she wished she could make into a soundtrack.

She rolled her body where it lay sprawled across Jason's and peeked at the olive-green cocktail dress. "Yeah, it came in yesterday. I'm wearing it to an art exhibit opening for a friend from college. And probably to my client's launch party at the end of the month." She had to donate some of her more fancy evening outfits she owned because they no longer fit, and she was in the midst of replacing them whilst trying not to offend her bank account.

"How's looking into opening up your own business going, by the way?"

"I haven't done anything beyond Pintresting what I think would be nice wallpaper. So pretty much just the fun stuff."

"Why?"

"Why I'm just doing the fun stuff and not the serious logistics?"

She felt him nod.

"I don't know. I'm busy with this campaign, and it's going to move me up in the company if I do well on it. For now, that's what I'm focusing on. Maybe in a few years I'll actually take the plunge."

They lay there quiet for a few moments. Jolene got so uncomfortable when she had to think about opening her own PR firm. It was something she'd always wanted to do once she understood that she enjoyed working in PR, but she had this recurring thought that she might meet epic financial and career failure if she tried. And any hopes of one day spearheading campaigns for major beauty companies and fashion shows were just fairy tales. It's why nobody knew about her dream except for Jason. She didn't know why her dreams felt safe when she discussed them with him. She hadn't known him nearly as long as she had Yvonne or even her sister.

"I couldn't do your job," he said.

"Why?"

"You have to attend too many events. I'd rather stay home and—"

"And watch boring documentaries," she finished for him.

He playfully squeezed her waist. "For your information, I also enjoy completing five-thousand-piece puzzles."

"It's a wonder how your mom and aunt get you gallivanting around the city attending all sorts of public events and activities."

He made a dismissive sound.

She chuckled. "Speaking of your mom, she invited me to your birthday dinner. The big five-oh, right?"

He swatted her backside.

"Hey," she said as she smiled. She'd been thrilled when Ms. Nadine had texted her about the dinner. She didn't immediately accept, deciding to run it by Jason before-hand, but she couldn't temper down the thrill she felt about sharing this little moment with him and those he cared about the most.

"She's convinced herself that we're dating."

"Well, I'd rather her think that than know what we're actually doing. So, should I RSVP?"

He was silent for too long, and Jolene frowned. Was she being too forward? Maybe this crossed the bounds of their relationship. It made her antsy that he might be trying to find a nice way to let her know that it did.

"I share a birthday with my dad," he finally said.

She felt her heart jerk.

"I understand if you'd prefer to spend it with just your family."

"No, I want you to come."

"Okay," she said, kissing his hand before propping her chin on his chest to look at him. "Tell me about him."

He looked at her, and she thought he might decline or change the subject, but he said, "He was the perfect complement to my mom. You see how vibrant and ener-getic she is? He was the same. He was funny and goofy. He would come home for work, and I would be doing my homework at the kitchen table, and without fail, he would kiss my mom and then give me this huge bear hug like he'd not seen me in weeks."

Tenderness rumbled through her.

"He liked rugby." He laughed a little bit. "A lot. He'd promised we'd play a full-contact game once I grew bigger."

She couldn't imagine how it must feel to lose a father that young. The need to wrap her arms around him and take that pain away was so strong that it shocked her. She didn't know if he wanted to be smothered in all that affection, so she clenched her fists to prevent herself from doing just that.

"It almost killed my mom losing him. Probably would've if I hadn't been there depending on her."

Jolene stroked his chest. He was far away now. But she stayed there, not really pulling him out of his thoughts.

"I should go," he abruptly said after several minutes had passed. He got up from her bed.

"Oh, okay."

"I know we had plans to watch that Netflix comedy special, but I forget I had something to do. Maybe some other time?"

He had already started to put his clothes back on. Jolene had to force herself not to ask him what it was, because Jason wasn't the type to just "forget" something he had to do. She kicked herself for bringing up memories that were painful for him. This thing they had going on was supposed to be fun and convenient, not an emotion excavation. He made his way to the door like the devil chased him, and she trailed behind him with her bed sheet wrapped around her body.

He got to the door and turned. "I'm sorry." He kissed her.

"Don't apologize. We'll talk later."

He walked toward the elevators. "See you," he said.

"Love——" She coughed, trying to distort what had almost escaped her mouth. She slammed the door shut and leaned heavily against it, not waiting to see if Jason had registered her flub.

Crap.

In the past, Jolene's instincts would've been to ignore the possible consequences and jump in feet first. Her ex-husband had been the same way. That's what drew them to each other. Their magnetic pull didn't give them a chance, however, to see the relationship for what it was: an ill-fated union between two people who might've cared for each other but whose passions greatly diverged. Toby had wanted to live out of a suitcase and never stay in one place for long, but Jolene had been determined to finish college and explore her own interests. To make the relationship work would've meant one of them abandoning their goals.

Now, Jolene couldn't stand the thought of destroying what she had with Jason because she once again got caught up in the beautiful details instead of acknowledging the bigger picture. She had grown to like Jason as a person, more than she could have thought possible. But regardless of the words that had wanted to spring forth so easily from her lips, she wasn't in love with him. He'd just finished pouring out little pieces of his heart, so of course she would feel somewhat emotional.

Satisfied that she wasn't really in love with Jason, she pushed herself off the door and headed to get into the shower. Thankfully, she hadn't had the opportunity to ask him to attend her friend's solo art exhibit in a few days. She needed the space, if only to further clear her mind.

Chapter 21

JOLENE QUICKLY SWIPED another delicious hors d'oeuvre from a server passing by. The gallery was full, and people were mingling and pensively commenting on her friend Mary's work that decorated the high expansive walls. Jolene shuffled along, realizing regrettably that her heels were too high for her.

"It's quite remarkable how Miss Garcia's paintings are so suggestive but simultaneously intimate," one fellow patron standing beside her said.

Jolene wasn't sure if the man directed the comment at her, but she nodded and pursed her lips. She tilted her head to the side and studied the array of colors and bold lines. One might assume Jolene was the artist with the way she smiled every time she overheard someone say something positive about the paintings. The obvious artistry impressed Jolene, even though she couldn't articulate exactly what she looked at or why it rivaled the best.

She briefly wished that Jason were here, if only to have someone to rave to about the really tasty food floating around the room. However, she had reduced how much she contacted Jason in the past few days, determined to create some distance. But the mental fortitude it took not to text him made her brain itch and her skin feel tight. She had too many screenshots in her camera roll that she'd hoarded trying to space out the time between her texts, and she also attempted not to dwell on how infrequently he messaged her as well. He was probably busy with work.

Jolene spotted her friend in the corner talking to an older woman. She pushed thoughts of Jason to the back of her mind and slowly slinked her way toward the pair. Mary's blond hair, fashioned into some oversize beehive, stood out amongst the crowd.

"Jojo," Mary said as she turned away from the older woman she spoke with to hug Jolene. "Thank you for coming."

"It's no problem, you're so talented. And your work is beautiful."

Mary gave her a charming pout and hugged her again. "Come meet my friend, Greta."

The older woman had stood there patiently as the two had greeted one another.

"Greta, this is my dear friend from college, Jolene Baxter. She's a fantastic PR manager; she actually introduced me to my fabulous web designer."

Greta nodded.

"And Jolene this is Greta Delaney, editor-in-chief of *Cashmere & Pearls* magazine."

Jolene was a little professionally awestruck. The woman was legendary in the world of media and entertainment. Greta had worked several jobs early-on in her career: radio, television, and editorial work, before making a leap into starting her own very successful and prestigious magazine.

"It's so nice to meet you, Ms. Delaney," Jolene said, trying to keep herself from fawning over the poor woman.

"Yes, and please call me Greta."

God. It was as if she'd stepped into someone else's life. The three women talked about the artwork surrounding them before naturally transitioning into talking about trends they'd all been seeing in their respective industries in terms of the digital space.

"I require all my clients to get social media," Jolene said. "I think it's something businesses can't discount because, if used correctly, it can be a game changer."

"Do you get pushback?" Greta asked.

"Not usually. However, I sometimes get resistance—"

"Hello, ladies."

A voice that had come to be synonymous with irritation pummeled through the women's conversation. Jolene had to curb the instinct to swat at Mark who had snuck up on their trio. The other two women turned to him, and it became clear neither one of them knew who Mark was.

She contemplated pretending not to know the man either, but he had other plans.

"Jolene, it's nice to see you. Will you introduce me to your friends?"

Annoyed but unwilling to make a scene in front of a legend in the magazine industry and mar Mary's special night, Jolene said, "Mark Timothy, Greta Delaney and Mary Garcia."

"Oh, Mark Timothy like Denis Timothy's son?" Greta asked.

"Yes. The one and the same," Mark replied as he threw his shoulders back.

"Your father was so generous renting out this space to me so last minute."

"It's a wonderful exhibit. More than worthy of this locale," Mark said.

Mary beamed at him, and Jolene wanted to throw up. Of course, it wasn't her fault, she didn't know what a tool Mark was.

"Yes, *Cashmere & Pearls* did a profile on your father a few years ago. Interesting man," Greta added.

The conversation lulled then, and Jolene opened her mouth to excuse herself when Mark said, "It's so good to see successful women supporting one another."

The women murmured their agreement.

"Sometimes I get jealous over how friendly you girls are with one another. No room for the guys," Mark continued, bumping his shoulder into Jolene's. "Isn't that right, Jojo?"

He delivered the words teasingly, but Jolene almost sneered. She held herself together by taking a swig of her champagne. Greta and Mary exchanged uncomfortable looks.

"How do you two know each other?" Greta asked. Her eyes lost the warmth they had when Jolene first met her.

"Friends and work associates," Mark said.

Maybe because the champagne was hitting her just right, Jolene said, "Yes, friends. If your definition of a friend is a person who doesn't know or respect your boundaries."

Mark let out a hearty laugh and patted her on the back like she was choking on something. None of the women laughed.

"I'd like you to leave," Mary said to Mark.

And Jolene felt the air get stuck in her throat.

Mark looked amused but didn't argue. He straightened his cuffs and turned to walk to another group that congregated in front of one of Mary's pieces.

"No, Mr. Timothy," Mary called out to him. "I mean, I'd like you to leave the event." Jolene's eyes widened, and she couldn't really feel her feet on the ground.

Mark approached the trio once more. "Are you serious, Miss Garcia?"

"Yes. Very. I can even call security to escort you out, if you want."

In that moment Jolene didn't know what Mark would do, but as the poster boy for charm and nice teeth, she should've known he wouldn't be caught acting an obvious fool in public.

Before he made his final turn to leave the gallery, he leaned heavily into Jolene's side and said, "Consider your access to my show revoked."

Jolene gave him a phony smile, raised her champagne glass, and made a toast. "To no longer being work associates."

He left the venue then, leaving the women in his wake. They didn't speak on the matter further, and half a dozen other people joined them. Small talk and artsy-fartsy conversations ensued.

The interaction with Mark had left Jolene feeling drained. After only an hour, she sent a quick text to an otherwise engaged Mary, thanking her again for the invite and getting rid of Mark. She said her goodbyes to the people around her and headed outside to wait for an Uber.

"Miss Baxter," Greta said, catching up to Jolene. "It was very nice meeting you."

"Yes, it was so nice meeting you too."

Greta offered her hand with a business card between her fingers. "Please reach out when you have a client you think would fit the *Cashmere & Pearls* brand. That's my personal phone number and email."

A little shocked, she took the business card. "Thank you, Greta."

The woman nodded and walked back into the throng of people like some guardian angel.

Take that, Fuck Face Mark.

"Which brand of pasta sauce do you prefer?" Jolene asked as she stared at the assortment of jars.

Jason had invited her over to his place to make up for how he'd abandoned her two weekends ago when all his feelings bubbled to the surface. The feelings he only let surface with his therapist and occasionally with his family. There was no reason to open up so thoroughly to someone who couldn't be in his life in that capacity for too much longer.

He'd been silent for a while when Jolene held up two options of generic pasta sauces to his face.

His lips turned downward in mild distaste. "No, we'll get some fresh tomatoes, oregano, Italian seasoning, fennel seeds, some garlic cloves—"

"All right, Chef Bobby Flay," she said, putting the jars back in their place. "I'm just used to dumping the cheapest jar of pasta sauce over overdone pasta after I come home from work. I meant no offense."

He chuckled and relaxed a little. He'd been concerned that she might be cold or annoyed with him for not texting her throughout the week in addition to bailing on her.

"How has work been?" he asked.

"Oh, oh, oh. You know how I met Greta Delaney last weekend. Well, I emailed her to thank her again and tell her it was nice meeting her. I didn't think she'd reply, but she did and asked if I wanted to get coffee in the near future and cc'd her assistant to set up a date."

"Hey now"—he lifted his hand for her to high-five —"that's a great contact you can use when you start your business."

She rolled her eyes but returned his high-five. "That won't be for many years."

She brushed off his interest in her career aspirations a lot. He previously thought it was because they weren't close like that, but the more he got to know Jolene, the more he suspected she did it because she actually didn't like the vulnerability that came with sharing lofty goals.

"You'll be a success." He, of course, didn't know this for certain, and he wasn't in the habit of making empty reassurances, but it nevertheless left his mouth. And it had the desired effect when her previously tense expression softened.

Jason led them down the frozen food aisle, searching for vegetables that wouldn't look anemic once steamed.

"I hope so. Also, I can start building my own connections that don't rely on the Able & Quinn name to get me in. I can be selective and not work with people like Mark."

"Wait, has he been causing you more problems?"

"Oh, has he ever."

She casually ran down confrontations she'd had with Mark and injected her usual humor and flippancy, but he couldn't tell if it was authentic or one that she adopted because she wanted to dispel his concerns.

"Does he know where you live?" he asked gruffly.

She looked a little taken aback by his question. "No, but I'm ninety percent sure he's the vindictive type that makes working life hellish as opposed to the type that cuts people up into small pieces."

He let out a harsh breath. "If you even feel a hint of fear, can you at least let me know?"

"Okay."

The way she bit her lip, Jason could tell that she resisted the urge to tease him. Which was a good thing because he was on the verge of suggesting she move into another place.

Like mine.

Wait, no, not his. The last time he'd lived with anyone was in college and that had been a nightmare. He did well in his own space and liked the control he had over the cleanliness and food in his apartment.

"So, tell me how it makes sense that you insist on homemade pasta sauce, but frozen vegetables are all right?" Jolene asked as she stared at the frozen packets he'd placed in their cart.

They arrived at a checkout line with one person ahead of them.

"I'm an enigma," he said as he gave her a quick kiss on her temple. It was the first time he'd publicly been affectionate with her, but it had come so naturally that he hadn't thought about it. When she didn't balk at the contact, he brushed any misgivings away.

"What's up, Jason?"

Jason looked up from loading their groceries onto the conveyor belt to see Anthony working behind the counter as one of the store's cashiers.

"Hey, man, what happened to McDonald's?" Jason asked.

Anthony ran an item's barcode and placed it into a plastic bag. "This pays better." He flashed a smile. "I got a last-minute interview."

"Cool, how's your summer going otherwise?" Jason

asked, aware that Jolene stood beside him, watching their interaction.

The young man shrugged. "It's been all right. I didn't make the first cut for the science competition."

"Damn, I'm sorry." Jason wished he could turn this loss around and miraculously make things better.

"It's okay. I still have my senior year." Anthony nodded toward Jolene. "Is this your girl?"

Jolene laughed. "No. A friend. Jolene." She offered her hand for Anthony to shake.

Anthony took her hand and smiled. "Nice to meet you."

If the smile that Anthony was sending Jason's way was any indication, the kid didn't believe the "friend" moniker. While their transaction processed, Jolene did most of the small talk, and Jason was amazed once again at how easy and effortless mingling was for her. Jason also tried to figure out why the idea of Jolene being his, legitimately and officially, simultaneously warmed him and made a sharp pang of anxiety settle in his stomach.

Once their groceries were paid for, Jason nodded to Anthony. "I'll see you after summer break. Stay out of trouble."

Jolene browsed his vinyl collection as he stored the leftover food they had for dinner. She'd called his lasagna "incredible," and he'd actually blushed. It was like the previous compliments he'd received from roommates, family, and all the other people he'd ever cooked for had been suspect until she'd confirmed it. He felt off balance by his response to her. The version of himself that he was with Jolene was foreign but oddly comfortable.

The whole reason his arrangement with Jolene existed was because he'd wanted to get out of his comfort zone and perhaps find some sort of movement in his stale life. Mission fucking accomplished because he now hurtled toward something he couldn't identify or control.

"How long have you been volunteering with the after-school program?" she asked.

He peeked into his living room where she crouched in front of his shelf.

"Three years. One of my patients is a program coordinator. They needed volunteers a few years ago, and it got me thinking about how I would've appreciated that type of program when I was younger. And so, I just decided to do it."

"I always forget that even though you come off as perfect, you haven't had a perfect life."

Jason drew closer to her. "Don't feel sorry for me."

"I don't."

"Good." He reached above her head to pull out the vinyl of Stevie Wonder's *Songs In the Key of Life*, and showed it to her.

"Oh my God." She grabbed the record from him to study the cover art.

He knew she liked seventies music, and if he didn't already own a lot of the albums of popular artists from the era, the glee on her face at that moment would have had him running to Amazon to make several purchases.

He took the record from her hands and placed it in the player. "Which song?"

"Let's go with 'Sir Duke' first."

The sound of braggadocios horns in the intro filled his living room, and Jolene's face broke into a smile. Then Stevie's voice came, and Jolene sang, adding her adorably off-tune vocals while she grooved to the music.

"Your neighbors are going to hate you!" she said over the loud music.

"They won't believe it's me."

She laughed and grabbed his hands so he would move with her. His objections died on his tongue, and he stopped resisting once he saw that she would just continue to move his stiff arms if he didn't just surrender. He mimicked her relaxed fluid motions and mimed air trumpets when they came in. He lost himself in the music and also sang with his decent voice holding the melody that Jolene's didn't care to.

She twirled into the next song and at one point even tripped over the corner of his rug but caught herself. She posed as if the whole thing was part of intricate choreography. He let out a laugh that left his cheeks and abs aching, and she turned to him long enough to smile a fetching smile that was all teeth and mirth. She didn't stop moving her body and even added some current dance crazes, but she wasn't trying to be sexy or even funny. The moment circled its way through his body. Pulling on strings and memories and dormant hopes and dreams until a light, buoyant feeling settled within him.

He was falling in love with Jolene.

The realization all but took his breath away, and he stopped dancing so abruptly that Jolene took notice and stopped as well.

She reached for him. "What's wrong?"

This was the same woman he'd been dancing with a few moments ago, but everything was different now. He stared at her for a few beats. The music continued to drone on in the background.

With her hand grasping his forearm, he forced the next words from out of him. "I don't think our arrangement can go on." He delivered the line mechanically with precision, like he told patients about the shitty side effects of certain prescription medicines.

She let go of his arm and looked at him, the worry that had pressed her brows melted away and was replaced with a more neutral expression. "Where's this coming from?"

How did he let himself start to care like this? He studied her closely. Was she starting to care for him in a different way than she cared for him as a friend? God, he wanted that to be the case, so maybe their arrangement had a chance to morph into something more…serious.

"Look at us, Jolene. We're dancing and laughing in my living room." He rubbed his face. "I don't do that." Knowing he had to be honest with her and himself. "This is no longer casual for me."

"I see."

She had convinced herself in the last couple of weeks she could do this thing a while longer. All she had to do was talk her feelings into submission, but she now stood in Jason's living room and he told her that he had feelings for her (or at least that's what she thought he said). She had to control the thrill that ran through her at the idea of him liking her beyond the stiff parameters they had created for themselves.

Besides, she wasn't ready or willing to investigate the feelings she may or may not have for Jason. The biggest project in her career currently needed her complete attention. Maybe they could revisit the conversation at a later date. This arrangement was supposed to be a fun distraction, but all the thoughts tumbling through her head were not pleasant. Damn him.

"So, what you're saying is that the clownfish and

anemone aren't helping each other out anymore." She knew her attempt to diffuse the awkwardness failed when Jason just looked at her.

"What I'm saying is that I like you."

"I like you too. That's what makes this"—she gestured between them—"perfect. Why change that right now?"

"We obviously want different things."

She could feel him shutting her out, and she wanted to undo everything. She had fun with him and not just in a sexual context. And maybe that was enough for some people to build lasting romantic relationships from, but Jolene needed more assurance. She needed to take her time because she'd seen firsthand that mere attraction and rapport did not make a relationship worth exploring. She just remained there looking at him, feeling the bile churn in her stomach.

"Yes, we do."

He silently walked over to where she'd dumped her duffle bag when she'd arrived. "I'll walk you out, then."

Jolene's heart shifted to some sort of painful place. She wanted to linger here for as long as possible because she knew deep down that though their relationship wouldn't return to the weird hostile one that existed just a few months ago, it would be as distant.

"Jojo." It sounded like a plea.

"Let's stay friends," she said almost desperately.

He averted his gaze. "Sure."

The bland acceptance irked Jolene. She could sense he held back. He wanted to get something off his chest.

Her heart rate sped up. "Say it," she said.

"Say what?"

"That thing you want to say. Just say it."

For a moment she thought he would just ask her to

leave, but then he said, "Why haven't you taken the plunge and started your PR business?"

She took a step backwards as if she'd been pushed. "What? Where is this coming from?"

"It's just"—he took a breath—"you feel deeply. I see it. *I* feel it. But you stop yourself from acting on anything real because…you're scared."

She made a sound that was a cross between a harrumph and a laugh. "Okay? And what does this have to do with our relationship, our friendship?"

"I think it's related."

The record player skipping was the only sound left after Jason stopped speaking. How long had it been doing that? The hiccupping sound matched Jolene's disbelief that the moment had devolved to this. She wanted to go back to them dancing in his living room, but instead, she now knew what he really thought of her. He thought she was a coward. She stared at him for a long time and he at her.

"You keep assuming you know me more than you actually do," she said, her voice hoarse like her internal screaming had actually affected her.

"I—"

She cut him off. "No, I'm good. I don't need a guy whose social circle only includes three people, to psychoanalyze me."

She wanted the comment to hurt, but he just smiled wryly.

"Tell me I'm wrong, then."

She stepped up close to him and tilted her head to meet his gaze. She wasn't touching him, but she wanted him to see her anger, feel it radiating from every pore. "Fuck you."

"We're no longer doing that, remember?"

She grabbed the duffle bag from his hand and walked

out of his apartment. He followed close behind her. She got into the elevator, and he entered it with her.

"What are you doing?"

"It's late. Let me walk you to your car," he said softly, the fire in his eyes temporarily dissipated. Of course, the always-perfect Jason Akana tried to be responsible even with all the emotions between them.

She straightened her spine. "I don't need you to."

He didn't respond, and she didn't have the energy to fight him on it. The elevator closed and took them down to the lobby of the building. He escorted her all the way outside but stopped well before she got to her car. She didn't turn around to say anything else. She couldn't say anything else, lest she burst into tears. She drove off and only let the tears flow when she arrived home.

Chapter 22

It was a Saturday afternoon, and Jason had just dropped off his aunt at her place and now drove his mom back home, where he planned to complete some tasks around the house.

"I didn't like the instructor today," his mother said from her place in the passenger seat.

She and Aunt Liza had joined a modern dance workout class at the community center. He responded with a grunt.

"You know how I hate those radio songs," she said.

She continued to prattle on about trivial things until they entered the house. He hadn't contributed much, but that didn't seem to bother or stop her. He removed ingredients from the fridge to make his mother a post-workout smoothie.

"Jolene called me this week to cancel her RSVP to your birthday—"

It was the first thing Jason had really registered the entire day. Hearing Jolene's name come up as if she hadn't dropped off the face of the planet like it felt she had, left him momentarily speechless. He wished he had social media just so he could feel some sort of tether, however slight, to her.

"Did she say why?" he finally asked.

His mother looked at him curiously. "She said something had come up that she couldn't get out of."

He nodded and continued to assemble the blender.

"Did you break up?"

He closed his eyes and let his head flop to his chest. "We were never dating."

"It didn't seem like that. You were close."

"Friends." He dumped some frozen fruit and protein powder into the blender.

"So, you're not friends anymore?"

He thought about how they ended it. Had it only been a week and a half ago?

"What did you do?"

He had to laugh past the needling guilt over what he'd said to Jolene that night. "Nothing, Mom. We're busy people and not as compatible as friends."

His mother shrugged. "She was good for you. She pulled you out of your shell...but I understand if she's not the one."

The sound of the blender paused their conversation, and Jason watched the ingredients combine and transform into maroon slush that ran smoothly against the blades. He missed the droning noise when it stopped.

"You two remind me of your father and me."

Jason clenched his jaw against a reaction. "You and Dad were perfect for each other. I never saw you two fight once." If marriage and kids were to ever come into Jason's life, his parents' short time together would be the prototype of an ideal relationship.

His mom let out a humored grunt. "You're a heavy

sleeper, and you also see the time we had with your father with rose-tinted glasses."

He handed her the smoothie in a glass.

"We fought. Over little things, over big things, and don't get me wrong, we loved each other, but it took effort to keep the peace."

He sighed. He didn't want that if that was the case. He'd worked hard all his life. Through sheer grit he'd sculpted a life for himself and his mother that was comfortable, and he didn't need the chaos of a tumultuous relationship disrupting that.

He knew his mother thought her anecdote would have the opposite effect, but it confirmed to him that he wanted the simple life and simple love without complicated trimmings. Maybe Jolene had done him a favor when she rejected a more serious relationship with him. Hopefully with time, he wouldn't feel so...sad.

He'd gone long without saying anything when his mother cradled his face in her cold hand and looked at him for another moment, as if seeing everything—the turbulent feelings he had for Jolene and how much effort it took to maintain an ideal life.

"You want everything to fall perfectly into place, my love. That's not how people work."

"I know that."

"Then grab onto happiness where it finds you. Stop debating whether it's what you initially had in mind."

"It's not that simple." He paused, debating how honest to be with his mother. "She doesn't want me."

She was silent for a moment. "Then you'll find another."

He thought that his mother would go into another bout of sage wisdom, but instead, she said, "I'm going to watch some Netflix while you fix that shelf."

It was the last push before the launch party in two days. Jolene and her team were holed up in a conference room on a Thursday evening. The room smelled like the Chinese takeout they had for dinner. One intern added rocks to tall vases that would work as decorative pieces for the moderately sized venue space the party would be held in. Another intern assembled gift bags that guests would receive at the end of the night.

Meanwhile, Jolene slid into panic mode as she looked at the growing list of things she needed to do. She'd been having nightmares for the last week where she was unable to get inside the locked venue and the event fell into disarray. Think plates breaking, the DJ playing the wrong setlist, and Jessica starting a food fight. Pasta may have been involved.

"Jolene, we've run out of the clarifying mist for the gift bags," an intern, Trudy, said from her place on the conference room floor. Jolene looked at Trudy and actively tried to process what she said while her brain spun to find a solution.

The sound of glass hitting tile came from outside, a few moments later a member of Jolene's team sheepishly poked his head into the room.

"Good news and bad news. Bad news I broke three of the vases trying to get them to my car. Good news, no one was hurt."

Todd, a hardworking and kind guy, emerged from behind his computer. "Did Robby ever confirm that the venue has the correct adapter the DJ needs?"

And in some bizarre Rube Goldberg-esque moment, a new email from Robby, the owner of the space that they were renting out for the launch party, popped up onto

Jolene's screen. All she read was the subject line: SET-UP TIME CHANGE FROM 3 TO 4 PM.

A little, frenzied laugh tickled the back of her throat, but she steeled herself against panicking. With the fortitude and the cool you might learn at overpriced spiritual retreats, she tackled each of the issues her team hurled at her in the span of fifteen minutes.

When she finally got the machine running smoothly once again, Jolene snuck away to the washroom, a place that in recent months seemed like some restorative sanctuary for her to go.

Two more days. Two more days.

"Jojo?" Yvonne said, coming into the restroom.

Her best friend found her hunched over the sink.

"Oh God, are you going to throw up?"

Jolene straightened. "No, I'm fine."

Yvonne drew closer until she leaned against the counter. "You're doing a good job."

She looked at her best friend, giving her an appreciative smile. She'd battled the feeling of inadequacy ever since—well forever, but this project and her recent "break up" with Jason had ramped it up.

"No, I'm serious. Able threw this project at you, and you've created such an amazing PR campaign. The launch party is bigger than we previously estimated and the presales for the fall boxes are outperforming."

She exhaled like Yvonne had given her permission to. "I promise to gloat once this is all over."

"Yeah, then you can help me plan my proposal to Di."

Jolene nearly jumped out of her skin. "You're finally doing it?"

Yvonne's dark lashes fluttered, and her cheeks grew red. "Yeah, I've been thinking about it for a while, and I even have a few rings that I've been looking at."

"You didn't tell me!" Not that Jolene expected Yvonne to relay every detail of this really intimate and decidedly private part of her life, but Jolene did expect Yvonne to relay every detail of this really intimate and decidedly private part of her life.

"We've been busy and besides, you've been really upset about—"

Jolene silenced her friend with a sharp slash in the air with her hand. Jolene had been more grateful for work at this moment than any point in her life because not only could she maintain her livelihood, but also, she was too busy to contemplate Jason for long periods of time. There were moments that he would spring up in her mind, and it felt like a rubber band had snapped on the back of her neck. But Jolene didn't have the time to recognize or mull over the sting, the lingering memory, and that suited her just fine.

"Stop. You don't need to protect my emotions. Let me relish in something good."

Yvonne looked hesitant for a beat before she pulled out her phone to show Jolene a series of rings, each one more beautiful than the next. Jolene could feel herself getting giddy, and she might have let out a squeal or two. All the stress from the last few weeks and months momentarily became background noise.

"This one," Jolene said, pointing to a stunning sterling silver ring with three dainty diamonds. "It's so Diana. Oh my God."

Yvonne hugged her. "I can't believe I'm picking out my future wife's ring in our work restroom."

Jolene laughed. "Potpourri will be a memory trigger to one of the most important moments in your life."

"There's a joke in there somewhere."

"Oh, I'm saving it for my reception speech."

Jolene had been running around all day, and her shapewear had become her mortal enemy. Other than that inconvenience, things had fallen into place despite having an hour less to set up.

The music the DJ played was chill without being lethargic. The lush and earthy tones of the decorative elements, in addition to the setting summer sun, suited the message and theme Essential Essence Apothecary tried to convey. People were using the party's social media hashtags and taking pictures in the aesthetically pleasing venue space.

Jolene made sure to greet everyone she passed and paid special attention to the selected figures from the press, including popular bloggers.

"People are raving about the bruschetta," Yvonne said, coming to stand beside Jolene at the side of the room. "And I heard Carmen and Jessica talking to Bev Styles from Maven Elite and she seemed impressed."

Jolene smiled. "The stations were a good idea too." Jolene nodded toward the interactive booths that had been set up to demonstrate how some of the products at Essential Essence were made.

"We're not even halfway through the night but I feel like we've done a good job," Yvonne said.

Jolene quickly knocked on the wood wall paneling. "No need to jinx it." But with that being said, Jolene allowed herself to recognize the little buzz that told her she was indeed pulling off this launch party. She vowed that when the party officially ended, she would think about how its success would help her get bigger accounts to lead. But for now, she looked upon what she and her team had succeeded in creating.

"Is that my phone or yours?" Yvonne asked.

Jolene looked down at her phone. "Mine." The number was unknown, but she answered it anyway. "Jolene Baxter."

"Hello, Jolene?" came a faint voice from the other side.

Jolene pressed the phone more firmly to her ear and looked for a spot with less noise. "Hello, who's speaking?"

"Jolene. It's Nadine Akana."

"Ms. Nadine?" Jolene's heart leapt. "Is everything okay? Is it Jason?"

"No, no. Jason is fine."

Jolene frowned. The woman wasn't the type to call her out of the blue. They'd communicated infrequently, and when they did, it was usually through text.

"I would've called Jason, but he's currently flying back from a conference. And Elizabeth is visiting her husband's family this weekend."

Jolene was even more confused now.

"I've hurt myself. It's just a sprained ankle but—"

"Stay on the line, Ms. Nadine. I'm on my way." Jolene retraced her steps to Yvonne. "I have an emergency. I need to leave. Can you take it from here—"

"Jolene!" Jessica shouted from a few meters away.

Jolene could tell from Jessica's quick determined steps and the way she waved her paper plate in the air that a complaint of some kind was imminent.

"My phone just died, and my speech is on it," Jessica said.

Yvonne and Jolene glanced at one another. Jolene had told both Carmen and Jessica to print off their speeches for this very reason. Nevertheless, this problem wasn't hard to fix.

"Go. I can handle this," Yvonne said quietly. "Call me when you can."

"Where are you going? I need—" Jessica called out.

Jolene heard Yvonne intercept, but she was already too far away to make out what was said. She cast aside the guilt she felt for leaving her event early and got into her car. She put her phone on speaker and placed it in the car's cup holder.

"Ms. Nadine, what happened? You should call the ambulance."

"It's silly. Not an emergency. I tried to reach some books on a shelf. I usually use a little stool, but when I went to step down, I rolled my ankle."

Ms. Nadine continued to describe her journey of crawling toward her cell phone to call for help. Jolene's heart rate didn't begin to slow down until she saw the older woman. She entered the house with the spare key Ms. Nadine revealed she kept under a small figurine of a Catholic saint beside her house.

"It's nice to see you, love," Ms. Nadine said from her place propped against the coffee table. "Oh God, were you at an event?" Ms. Nadine asked, taking in Jolene's dress and pinned hair.

"Don't worry about it."

Jolene eyed Ms. Nadine's dangerously swollen ankle and had to ignore the anxiety that whirled in her. Jolene had a distant uncle, probably older than Ms. Nadine, who had fallen on his morning walk and broken his hip. It was the beginning of the end for him.

"You should've called the ambulance," Jolene said again, then she kicked off her heels to get a better traction as she hoisted the older woman up.

"It's a fuss. It's a sprained ankle for goodness' sake."

They slowly made their way toward her car. Only stopping long enough for Jolene to lock the front door behind them. Jolene tempered down the need to tell the woman her injury might be worse than just a sprained ankle.

"When does Jason's plane arrive? I'll call him as soon as he lands."

"No. Hold off until the doctor sees me. The boy will have an aneurism." She paused. "Maybe you want him to drop dead."

Jolene gave Ms. Nadine a startled look, almost hitting her own head on the side of the car.

"No, I don't wish Jason any harm."

"Good. That's good," Ms. Nadine said. "But you're angry with him?"

"Why? Did he say something?"

"No," she responded too quickly.

"We had an argument, but I'm not angry," she said simply. And she meant it. She had tried to cling onto the anger and resentment she felt toward Jason for what he had said the last time they spoke at his apartment, but it quickly became exhausting to maintain.

Jolene somehow got the woman seated and buckled in the back of her car with her leg propped up on the seat beside her. She turned off the loud air conditioner, wanting to be present and receptive to any sounds of discomfort that Ms. Nadine might make. Neither of them said anything for a while.

"I really should move into a smaller place. Maybe a condo or townhouse," Ms. Nadine said.

"That's understandable."

"Not because I'm old or I don't like the house. It has wonderful memories, but it's so big, and it's just me there all the time."

Jolene didn't say anything, sensing the women simply thought out loud.

"He's going to try and manage me," Ms. Nadine said

under her breath, but Jolene heard it and knew Ms. Nadine referred to Jason.

"I usually just flip him off and keep it pushing." Why had she said that?

This was his mother and she expected to hear a harsh reply, but Ms. Nadine laughed. "That's a good one."

Ms. Nadine hissed.

"Are you okay?"

"Yes. I just bumped my foot."

Jolene cast a look at Ms. Nadine through the rearview mirror.

"No. No. No. I reject that look you're giving me, Jolene. Let the doctors worry about me. Tell me why you're dressed so nicely."

"A launch party for a client."

"I'm sorry I'm making you miss it. You can leave once you've dropped me off."

Jolene smiled, making eye contact with the woman in the mirror. "No, I'm glad you called. I'll have to call Jason, though, as soon as he lands. I can't leave him out of the loop, and I'll wait with you until he arrives.

Ms. Nadine didn't respond right away, and Jolene looked in the mirror, expecting the older woman to be irked, but instead, she looked amused and had a glint in her eye.

Finally, she said, "Of course, whatever you think you have to do."

Jason didn't know how many traffic laws he broke by the time he arrived at the hospital Jolene had taken his mother to. He had always been prepared for the worst in his life, but overwhelming dread hit him upon hearing that his mother had injured herself to the extent that she needed medical attention. The knowledge that Jolene accompanied his mother enabled him to operate with some sort of clear-mindedness.

"I'm here for Nadine Akana," Jason said, practically shouting at the nurse at the front desk of the emergency room.

Once verifying his relation, the nurse led him to a curtained-off room where his mother lay in a bed with her eyes closed. He tried not to superimpose the image of his father decades before in a similar bed in hospice.

"Jason," Jolene said as she appeared from nowhere.

She hugged him, and he wasn't sure if he hugged her back.

There was tightness in his neck and behind his eyes. "I can't lose her yet."

"Baby, you won't. She's fine. Just asleep"—she brushed tears from his cheeks he hadn't known had fallen—"they gave her some medication for the pain. She told me the whole way here how it was a sprained ankle, and the doctor confirmed it. They're keeping her here for a few hours to monitor her response to the pain medication since she's a little older."

He looked at Jolene for the first time. Really registering her presence.

"Thank you," he said.

She soothingly massaged his temples, and he relaxed a fraction. They stood there, her arms encircling him as they swayed back and forth. After several minutes, she quietly said, "Sit down. She's bound to wake up soon. I'll go get you something to drink."

Jolene disappeared, then, and Jason sat on the chair beside his mother's bed and held her hand in his, running his fingers over the faint freckles and veins he found there.

It had been him and his mom for so long, and he had worked really hard to secure them both, to pull them to a place where they didn't have to worry about money or the future.

"You worry too much," his mother said. He didn't know how long she'd been awake watching him.

"No, I worry just enough."

She dismissed his concern with a weak wave of her hand.

He clenched his jaw. "Mom, it's not safe for you to be in that house alone." He raked his hands through his hair. Maybe he should install some sort of panic alert system or perhaps his mom would be open to adopting a dog that could call for help with its paw.

"It was an accident. It could've happened even if a dozen people were in the house. You can't control everything."

He let out an exasperated laugh. "Yes, I know that. Life has shown that to me, time and time again, but I can mitigate risk, and having you in a house alone is clearly—"

"Jason Akana. I might need to be more careful, yes. But you will not treat me like you're the one who raised me. I won't allow it."

Thoroughly reprimanded, Jason kissed the back of his mother's hand.

"Jolene was very kind to come to my rescue. She even gave me a tip to handle you when you get like this."

Jason frowned. "You two were discussing me?"

"Hmm."

Jason would have to investigate what was said later on, but he relaxed a bit more seeing how normal his mother acted. Jolene's reappearance with a bottle of water and what looked like a bag of M&Ms cut their conversation short.

"Here," she said as she handed him the snacks.

"Thanks."

Then the three of them silently looked at each other, listening to the buzz of the machines, grasping for a safe topic they could all engage in.

"Where are your shoes?" Jason finally asked.

Jolene looked down at her feet clad in blue shoe covers. "At your mom's house."

"She had to take them off to help me up from the floor."

The image got him breaking into a cold sweat. His mom squeezed his hand.

"I have another pair in my car. They don't go with the outfit, but they'll do."

She wore the olive-green dress he'd seen hanging in her closet. He then remembered today was the day of her clients' launch party, and before he could ask her about it, the curtains that separated them from the bustling hospital's hallways opened, and a female doctor with a messy top knot and stethoscope slung around her neck entered.

Without looking up from her chart, she said, "Hi, I'm Dr. Bayuk, you must be Mrs. Akana's son."

It took Jason a little over ten seconds after the woman introduced herself and looked up to meet his gaze to place the name. By that point, she'd moved on to asking his mom how she felt.

"Bailey," he said out loud. The last name was the same as the elderly couple in his apartment complex, and she fit the blurry image that Mrs. Bayuk had shown him of her granddaughter on her phone.

Bailey smiled. "Yeah, I recognized your name as well."

It was as if they both simultaneously remembered the date he cancelled and the zero effort he had put in to reconnecting. He'd been a little busy falling for someone who didn't want a romantic relationship with him.

"I should let you all have your privacy," Jolene suddenly said.

"No, you can stay," his mom said.

"I should head back to my event anyway. I need to make sure it hasn't collapsed in my absence," Jolene said as she crouched low near his mother's face to hug her and whisper something in her ear.

"Let me walk you out," Jason said, moving past Bailey to the hallway where Jolene stood. He could be honest with himself and admit that part of him offered to make sure that a somewhat barefoot Jojo made it to her car without slicing her foot open, but he also wanted to extend his time with her.

"I'm fine. Stay with your mom." She looked a little gray, but could he blame her? She had just traversed the city trying to help his mother, and she missed a big chunk of her career-defining event.

"Thank you again," he said.

She patted his chest where his sternum lay. "You're a terrific son."

He found it hard to form words around the lump in his throat.

"Take care, okay?" she said before walking away.

He watched until he couldn't see her anymore.

Jolene's entire body shook by the time she entered her vehicle. She flexed then clenched the hand that had made contact with Jason's chest. Of course, she had expected to see him, but she hadn't meant to, couldn't have predicted the almost painful ache in her chest. He'd been so worried for his mother, and all she wanted to do was caress him and kiss his face.

The time it took her to fetch his water and candy, she'd convinced herself she could stop being the coward he had accurately guessed she was and just embrace the feelings he stirred in her. She could do it, even if she still couldn't pinpoint what those feelings were and despite how much they scared her.

She had made the decision that she would let him know she'd spoken too soon when she said she wanted things to remain casual. On Monday, after she made sure Ms. Nadine felt better, she'd planned to call him and let him know about her change of heart.

All her plans had flown out the window, however, the moment Dr. Bayuk had walked into the curtained-off room. She and Jason seemed to know each other, and there was a moment where they had a silent conversation. She noticed the spark of interest in Dr. Bayuk's, or *Bailey* as Jason referred to her, eyes. Its presence deflated all of Jolene's exuberance about possibly reconciling with him.

From the quick conversation she'd had with Dr. Bayuk before Jason's arrival, Jolene assessed the woman was bubblegum and sunshine whereas Jolene was more like those abrasive, hot, cinnamon, heart-shaped candies. Bailey's personality complemented Jason's mild demeanor more.

Jolene had so thoroughly convinced herself of this woman's worthiness, she could've taken the elevator up to the hospital's gift shop and bought the happy couple a congratulatory card and a gift basket.

But above all else, her reaction to Bailey and Jason's interaction, made it clear to her that she wasn't ready for anything romantic yet. She had doubts, not of Jason's suitability but of her ability to not screw things up. She thought she'd journaled and counseled her way through those insecurities after her divorce, and she assumed they became inconsequential after she landed her job at Able & Quinn. But they reared their ugly heads now, and how could she ask Jason to manage that? It would be the demise of the relationship sooner rather than later.

Chapter 23

THE MONDAY after Essential Essence's successful launch, Jolene had walked around her office with "Staying Alive" by the Bee Gees playing in a loop in her head. But now it had been a week, and she struggled to keep the optimism alive. She'd received no feedback from her bosses, and she hadn't been assigned another account to lead. She hid her impatience by putting her full effort into other tasks and assignments. For instance, this morning she'd sent several emails before she even got her first cup of coffee in.

"I love the skirt," a PR assistant said to Jolene when she hopped off the elevator.

"Thanks, Melanie."

The smile she had on her face from the early morning compliment died when she saw Mr. Able leaning against her office door. She hadn't heard anything from him since the off-boarding process for Essential Essence last week. She stopped short and quickly checked her phone to see if she had missed a notification for a meeting. There was nothing. It was unusual to see him in the office this early, but even more odd that he was on her side of the building. If he'd wanted to speak with her, he would've asked one of the receptionists to send a message or he would've sent her an email.

"Mr. Able, good morning."

Using his thick shoulder, her boss pushed himself off from where he leaned. "Miss Baxter, follow me please."

Shit. Okay. Very unusual, and her brain scrambled for a reason. Was she about to get promoted? That had to be it. Okay, maybe not a promotion but at least some sort of verbal confirmation she inched closer toward her goal.

When she entered his office, there was a woman in her fifties already seated. Jolene was a bit thrown off by her presence.

"Take a seat, Miss Baxter. This is one of our company lawyers, Denise Simmons," Mr. Able said.

A lawyer?

Jolene placed her work bag and purse beside her chair, sat on the edge of the seat, and clasped her hands together to force herself not to fidget. Mr. Able looked at something outside of his window, and she wondered how long it would take for him to actually speak.

"You're a good employee—"

"Thank you, sir."

"So, it's a shame that I have to do this." He turned away from the window, then, and walked to his desk, taking his seat. "Effective immediately, you no longer work for Able & Quinn."

Jolene knew words. She knew how they could be strung together to create sentences, and how those sentences could and oftentimes did have meaning, but for some reason she sat looking at her boss with a blank expression. She did not understand.

"I'm firing you, Jolene," he added gently, correctly

assessing that she hadn't fully taken in his previous statement.

"But—"

Was the company downsizing? God, had Jessica gone and told him that she'd left the launch party for a few hours? Everything had run smoothly in her absence, and she'd returned well before a big chunk of the guests had left.

Mr. Able continued to speak, and she knew the answers to her questions could be discovered there, but she couldn't make out what he said over the noise of her own thoughts. Mr. Able eventually nodded to Denise, and the lawyer handed her a folder.

"I'd like you to consider signing this release of liability. With it, you'll receive two weeks' severance pay," Mr. Able said.

Was this happening right now?

She signed the release, and Mr. Able offered his hand and Jolene limply placed hers in his and he moved it up and down. Denise did the same. She found herself in her office for the first time that day and for the last time ever. She just stared at her bulky furniture, the weight of the company laptop in her bag suddenly felt too heavy to bear. How'd this happen? She hiccupped as she unsuccessfully tried to catch the first tears that fell.

"Oh great, you're here. You weren't replying to my texts and—" Yvonne stopped short as she came into Jolene's office and saw her in the middle of the room.

"Girl, what's wrong?" Yvonne asked. She placed the papers she had walked in with on the desk.

Jolene looked at her friend. "I just got fired."

"What! Why?"

Jolene handed Yvonne the file, and Yvonne flipped through it.

"This is bullshit. This makes absolutely no sense."

"Can you help me pack my stuff?"

"Of course. I'll help you pack, and then I'll take the day off. We can mope then find a lawyer to fight this shit."

Jolene rubbed her face to rid herself of the tears that had fallen. She didn't care that she smudged her makeup.

"No, I already signed the release. And you're not taking a day off. Just help me pack and I'll call you either tonight or tomorrow."

Yvonne threw her arms around Jolene. "I'm here. And you'll get through this, okay?"

Jolene numbly nodded and accepted the comfort. Her mind worked in slow motion at the moment. But the upside to that was she was unable to truly internalize the pitying glances she got from her former coworkers as she exited the building with a box of her belongings.

"I was a total nerd. I went to band camp and everything," Bailey said.

Jason sat across from her in a dimly lit restaurant. This was technically their second date, their first happened accidentally when his mother was in the hospital over her sprained ankle. He'd taken his mom to the hospital cafeteria to grab something quick to drink after she'd been discharged, but she ended up abandoning him to chat with a woman she knew from some fitness class or another.

That's when Bailey, on her break, had come to his table and they'd talked. He'd apologized for cancelling their date, and they'd laughed about it, but she'd ended up asking him out after what turned out to be a pleasant conversation. His kneejerk reaction had been to decline. In the past this reaction would've been the result of his introversion, but now it had more to do with how he felt about Jolene. He had to move on, and Bailey was sweet and amiable.

"Nothing wrong with being a nerd. I think we make the world a little more fun," he said.

Bailey flipped her hair over her shoulder and giggled. "I always say I'm part of the solution not the *precipitate*."

"Ah, nope. I think that corny pun takes you to a nerd level I know nothing about," he said.

She laughed, and he did too, and he accepted that he presently enjoyed his time with Bailey. The waiter brought their food, and Jason slid his plate closer to Bailey to give her better access to it. But then it immediately struck him that he did that because he would've done that while dining with Jolene. She was the only person he knew who would want to steal bites of his food. Jason drew his plate closer to himself and felt his appetite wane.

"You don't like the food?"

Jason shook himself out of his trance and looked down at his untouched meal and back at Bailey. "No, it looks absolutely delicious." He dug into the food to confirm it. "Yup, delicious."

They ate their food mostly in silence but latched onto random topics when they sprung up. As their waiter cleared their dinner plates, a wave of applause swept through the restaurant. Jason turned to see the reason, and from his angle he could sort of make out that a woman was on her knee proposing to another woman. Jason smiled and offered a few claps in congratulation. He turned to Bailey and she was doing the same.

"How sweet. Hopefully one day," she said wistfully.

He nodded, thinking similarly.

"I didn't mean that to be a hint or anything," Bailey quickly added, her face and neck flushed. "Obviously."

Her comment made him pause because ideas of marriage and long-term partnership conjured an entirely different woman. And as pleasant as their dinner had been, it had felt hollow. It was for that reason he knew that this would be the last date he'd have with Bailey.

Jolene quickened her steps. She didn't want to be late returning from her lunch break. She was still new and subject to firing. One termination in her lifetime was enough. It was a new experience to actually have a lunch break and not sporadic minutes throughout the day when she could sprint to Starbucks for her daily hit.

Her first week as a receptionist at a realtor's office had taken some getting used to. She no longer answered the phone with just her name and title. She now represented the business and the people on the other line didn't much care who she was. The fact that she found a job a week after she was fired, with the assistance of Yvonne and Yvonne's cousin, helped Jolene not feel so hopeless and embarrassed about her situation.

She'd taken the first job available to her, because she didn't want to feel desperate while searching for a new position in her field. And despite her intentions to eventually find work that would pay for her lifestyle again, she eyed a cheaper apartment. If the job search took longer than she expected, the last thing she wanted to do was dip into her savings (her future business startup fund) to pay rent. She was coping as well as she could, but the cupcake store near her new workplace was the only change Jolene enthusiastically accepted.

In her hands, she shifted the box of cupcakes that she'd bought for the office and tried not to lose her footing on the uneven sidewalk. She planned to buy her new coworkers' adoration and respect with confectionaries. Upon rounding the corner to the stretch of offices that included hers, she was met with Mark making his way toward her. He hadn't noticed her, and for a split second, Jolene debated turning around or ducking behind the cars to her right till he passed.

She didn't know if he'd heard about her firing. It didn't matter, however, because regardless of whether he knew or not, she wouldn't give him the satisfaction of seeing her defeated or ashamed. She lifted her chin high and planned to pass him without a word.

Mark eventually looked up from his phone and made eye contact with her. "Jolene," he said when they finally were close enough.

She offered him nothing but silence. Her shoulders dropped as soon as she passed him, but from behind her, he continued to talk.

"I heard you were fired. That had to suck."

The smug way he said it was the only reason she stopped in her tracks. Today she had time. Well, she had exactly eight minutes to get back to the office, but she would spend at least thirty seconds of it telling Fuck Face Mark what she thought about him.

She spun around and looked at the man she would've described at one point as handsome, but a horned beast ascending from hell would be more appealing now.

Her chin rose even higher. "Listen, I don't know what you gain from gloating, but I hope it keeps you warm at night."

He gave her a smile that lacked any warmth. "I just find it funny how your meathead boyfriend tried to throw his weight around and it backfired."

Jolene's heart rattled in her chest. He had to be referring to Jason, but what did Jason have to do with anything? Mark and Jason didn't even run in the same circles.

Her confusion must've been evident because Mark said, "Oh, he didn't tell you that he was talking shit and it got back to me."

Jolene frowned. Jason wasn't the type to go out of his way to bad mouth someone. There had to be a mistake.

Unless.

If Jason was anything, it was honorable, and Jolene could see him protesting a compliment paid to Mark. The idea made her feel warm, and despite the current confrontation, the tightness in her body eased. "Yeah, bitterness is unbecoming, but good luck with life," Jolene said and turned away, ready to never see the asshole again.

"You know my father refers his clients to Able & Quinn sometimes."

Jolene continued to walk. She no longer cared.

"That type of relationship provides leverage for say"— he paused—"when you wish a particular person didn't work there anymore."

Jolene's steps faltered. She turned around once again to face Mark. She could see the truth in his eyes. He'd gotten her fired.

Her hands were tingling. What would it be like to wipe that smug look off his face by throwing a cupcake at it? The icing would definitely destroy his fancy suit.

"Careful there, Jojo, you're destroying your cupcakes," he said, gesturing toward where she squeezed the container.

She wanted to say something biting and cold, but all her mental functions were occupied with maintaining some level of calm. He walked away, as if dismissing her anger, her feelings, and she was left with only three minutes to get to her station before her lunch break was over.

She spent the remainder of the day in an angry haze. But she grinned through it. A sharp, Cheshire-Cat-like smile that she refused to let dim as she replayed her firing, as she recalled her interactions with Mark throughout the years, and as her new coworker, Tamara, corrected her on the mistakes she made. By the end of the day, Jolene was surprised to find her teeth hadn't shattered.

"Have a good evening now," Tamara said as Jolene walked to her car.

"Thanks, you too, Tamara."

Once Jolene got to her apartment, she let her anger loose. Through steps she hadn't really planned out but nevertheless felt compelled to do, Jolene dropped her things in the entryway and grabbed the abstract-shaped award that accompanied the bonus she received last year at Able & Quinn. She retrieved the hammer from the tool kit she'd bought on a whim months ago and hacked away at the award with steady blows.

⸻

"Earth to Jojo. Did you hear anything I just said?" her sister asked over Skype. Her face was pressed close to the screen.

It was later in the evening, during Jolene's weekly Skype call with her sister. She still needed to fully process her anger, but she was less in the mood to become some empress of destruction.

"Yes. Baby shower. Mom is going overboard. Worse than when you got married."

"Okay, but you're still clearly distracted. What's up?"

Jolene should be indulging her sister in this special moment in her life. Nicole had been sending her videos of her expanding belly and every small update from the way her hair flourished to the new stretch marks that had appeared on her thighs.

"No, it's nothing." Jolene didn't want to needlessly upset her sister by discussing what Mark had done. Nicky knew she no longer worked at Able & Quinn; that's all she needed to know for now.

"All right," Nicole said, moving her screen back so she wasn't so pressed up against the frame. "I'm going to run down possible issues. Tell me when I get to the one that's bothering you."

Jolene smiled. It was a technique their parents had used on them when they were stubborn teens who were less likely to divulge that they were sad about the sizes of their bodies and unrequited crushes.

"We don't have to do that. It's just that I'm still upset about getting fired."

"I know. It's going to be difficult. You might not make as much as you were making before, but look on the bright side, you can now search for something you actually like to do."

This jerked Jolene out of her stupor. "Wait, what? I loved my job."

"You did?" Nicole furrowed her brows. "I always thought it was something you fell into and just stayed there because it was convenient."

How could her sister not have seen how much Jolene had loved working in public relations? She'd put in so much time and effort into her career and in rising within Able & Quinn because she enjoyed doing what she did. Not to mention she was damn good at it. She might've fallen into the profession, but she discovered she was well suited to the socializing and relationship-building the job required.

Jolene shook her head. "It's definitely work I want to do for a long time."

Her sister was silent and studied her. "I had no idea." She let out a little laugh. "You rarely talk about it. Every time I ask you what you're doing at work you—" Nicky mimicked the way Jolene would shrug her shoulders and wave her hands dismissively.

Jolene rolled her eyes at her sister's exaggerated imitation of her and sunk back into her couch. She'd held back in sharing her actual interest and enjoyment in her job because she'd notoriously been noncommittal throughout her life. Whether it was failing to give gymnastics any serious attention or that time she'd abandoned learning to play the guitar after claiming to want to be the second coming of Jimi Hendrix. And let's not forget the marriage she'd called quits on. Sure, the divorce had been the right decision, but it had been one of many choices that had revealed a pattern. It made her cautious of vocally expressing interest or passion when it could very well not last. She felt a bit foolish now.

"So, you've been applying to other PR companies?" Nicole asked.

Jolene hesitated. She was once again about to brush off the interest with a lukewarm response. She'd been applying to other companies but without much enthusiasm. Other ideas consumed her.

She inhaled deeply. "Yes and no. I've been thinking about opening up my own PR business."

"Whoa. Okay. That sounds ambitious."

"It's going to happen."

There was a sort of a release and calm that settled within Jolene once she had revealed that.

"Jojo, that's amazing. I'll support you in whatever way I can."

For the remainder of their conversation, they meandered in and out of less serious topics, and Jolene felt champagne light. And after hanging up, the urge to text Jason invaded her mind. She wanted to let him know she'd finally committed to starting her very own PR business. She dashed the thought away immediately, however. Would he even care?

Yes.

It upset Jolene to know Jason would probably hear about her business coming to fruition through the grapevine. However, she couldn't dwell on that. To emphasize her resolve to no longer think of Jason as an intimate part of her life, she pulled out a loose-leaf paper and started a list that would help her make her dreams a reality.

Chapter 24

JASON SET the boxed cake that was more than half-gone on his counter before collapsing on his couch. He'd spent the afternoon with his family celebrating his thirty-sixth birthday. Thirty-six. He said the number out loud a couple of times. How the hell had he gotten here? He smiled as he recalled his mother's roundabout birthday toast that included embarrassing stories and fond memories.

His luncheon had been held at his aunt and uncle's home because his mom had decided she no longer wanted to live in his childhood home. The house was in chaos since she'd already started the packing process. She'd broken the news to him a few days ago in the same way someone might rip a Band-Aid off, really quick and without remorse.

She gave him the choice to move in if he wanted to. He expected to feel hurt or at least feel compelled to save the house that he'd fought to get back. But he didn't feel anything. Well, that's not true. There was something almost humorous about discarding something that had been emblematic of his success. But that was the thing: He'd been so loyal to his goals and achievements that he never stopped to question if they were what he wanted or, in this case, what his mom even wanted.

Part of Jason's motivation for repurchasing their house had been to regain a semblance of what they'd lost when his dad died, but it had also been his response to life throwing down the gauntlet. But his father's memory was more than a mere house, and he didn't want to hang onto the house just to prove he *could* do it. The pictures, the stories his extended family back in Tonga shared, and the times when his mother told him he looked so much like his father were the reasons Jason could now so easily let go.

Jason fixed his gaze on his father's record player. He hadn't used it since the night Jolene was at his place, but he got up now to put on his dad's favorite record to send him a happy birthday. The ringing from his phone stopped his progress, and the moment Jason answered it, the blaring sound of an air horn burst through the phone. He pulled the device away from his ear.

"Happy birthday!" Ty said after the loud honk ended.

"Thanks, man."

"Thirty-fucking-six."

Jason laughed.

"You good?"

Jason stretched out on his couch once again. "Yeah, why wouldn't I be? It's my birthday." He tried to inject some enthusiasm into his voice.

"You just sound off. Not that I expected you to be your usual bubbly, loud self, but—"

"Ha! I'm just tired. I spent the last few hours eating my weight in frosting. Give me a break."

Ty was silent for a while, and Jason could hear the cogs turning in his friend's head. What was he gearing up to say?

"So, nothing else?"

"No?"

There was another moment of silence.

"You obviously have something you think is on my mind, so spit it out."

"Man, I know you and Jolene broke up."

Jason made a protesting sound. "We were never together."

In spite of his claim, most days Jolene wasn't far from his mind. Whenever he thought he was getting over her, there'd be a commercial, a funny occurrence at work, or a song that would remind him that he wasn't in fact getting over Jolene. There was no escape from the hollow feeling, and it frustrated Jason how long this process was taking. But unless Ty had suddenly become clairvoyant, there was no reason for him to suspect that Jolene and he had a relationship beyond the bland one he'd witnessed several times before.

"Who told you that?" Jason asked.

"Okay, maybe you guys weren't *dating* dating, but it was clear that after the trip, something changed between you guys. You barely took your eyes off her the night you two arrived at our place, man."

Jason had stopped breathing at some point, but Ty continued speaking.

"Also, every time I've brought up Jojo in the last few months, you've gotten flustered. Ergo, you two have been...close."

Flustered would never be an adjective Jason would describe himself with. And if he wasn't feeling just that in that moment, he might have vehemently denied ever experiencing it.

"Our relationship, friendship, whatever you want to call it, was only meant to be casual. I'm fine with that.

More than fine with that," Jason said, even though he knew it was a lie the second the words left his mouth.

Ty let out a low whistle. "So, that's what you guys are doing?"

"What are you talking about?"

"It's just both of you happen to be miserable simultaneously, and you can't put two and two together."

Jason frowned. "Jolene's miserable?" The thought of her wallowing in her apartment instead of wearing some pretty party dress as she hypnotized everyone with her humor and spunk distressed him to an illogical degree.

"Well yeah, losing a friend and your job around the same time does that to you."

Jason's vision blurred for a several moments and everything slowed down. "Jolene lost her job?"

"Shit. I shouldn't say anything else, man. Nicky will have my neck. I had strict instructions."

"Ty, tell me."

The roughness in his own voice shocked him, and it was probably why Ty didn't brush off his request.

"I won't go into detail, but Jolene got fired last month. She was pretty much blindsided."

Jason's head swirled. From what his mom had told him, Jolene had nailed her launch event. This was supposed to be her steppingstone to bigger and better things. To her own PR business.

"Hey. Jolene's fine. She has a new job and everything."

Ty's reassurance didn't do much for Jason, because for the rest of their conversation he tried to decide if he should send her a text. The unfairness of it all made his chest ache. He'd seen her work hard throughout the months. He witnessed how animated she became whenever she talked about her job or the people she got to work with.

He got off the phone with Ty and continued his birthday night like he'd intended. But while he lay in bed, before drifting off to sleep, a thought shoved its way into his conscious, cruel and incessant.

Jolene getting fired was his fault.

The day of his mother's accident, he'd been flying back from a conference. The conference had been in some ways bureaucratic but mostly insightful. Jason had rubbed shoulders with some important people from across the country. He'd met Denis Timothy, a mogul whose company was a sponsor for the conference. He'd never met the man before, but Jason couldn't drop the feeling that he looked familiar. It wasn't until the two men were in the same group that Jason had made the connection.

The older man had stark white hair that gave him a Colonel Sanders look. He bragged about his son like many parents do, and something clicked in Jason's head that this was the father of the man who had been harassing Jolene, Mark Timothy. He hadn't planned to say anything because the older man had nothing to do with his son's actions.

"Very eloquent. Very intelligent," Mr. Timothy had said as their group discussed the scholar who'd done a presentation on immigration and health care.

It was as if the pistol had been already loaded and just waited for the chance to be shot because Jason said, "Same can't be said about your son."

Now, Jason couldn't speak to Mark's intelligence, but it had felt good to take a dig at the man's son even in a trivial way. Jason's comment didn't register in the larger conversation that continued around them, and Denis Timothy didn't react either. Jason wasn't even sure if the man had heard him. It was only when Mr. Timothy excused himself from the group that he spared Jason and Jason's nametag a glance.

He had forgotten about the incident almost immediately, but there was a chance that his slight toward Mark had reached him. Jolene had called the man vindictive. Could he be petty enough to get a woman fired over something a friend said in her defense?

She had to find another job because of me.

Swallowing the bile that rose, he sat up in bed. The idea that he might've derailed Jolene's career was near earth-shattering. If his life and more so the last few months had emphasized anything, it was that control was an illusion and maybe he shouldn't try so hard to maintain it, but bad habits die hard. He needed to find a way to fix the mess he'd created.

"No, I want magenta not purple," Yvonne said.

Jolene looked at the pack of fancy pens she'd placed in her shopping basket. "Girl."

"What?" Yvonne retrieved the pens, placed them back on the shelf, and picked up an eerily similar pack and held it for Jolene to see. "Magenta."

Jolene swallowed the teasing comment. Yvonne and Di had wasted no time between their engagement and the planning for their winter wedding.

"Nothing to say, huh?"

Jolene shook her head and mimicked locking her lips together.

"Amazing. I have to get married more often."

Jolene playfully bumped her as they continued down the aisle of the craft store.

"How's the new apartment?" Yvonne asked.

Jolene let out a noise that sounded like a poor imitation

of a wounded animal. "It's drafty. Not a big deal now, but winter is a thing. Also, the worst WiFi."

"My offer still stands; you can move in with Di and me for a bit. It'll give you time to find a place you like."

"No. I'm just being picky."

Also, Jolene wanted to stand on her own two feet right now. Prove that nagging voice in her head wrong that she was not a fuckup who needed pity and coddling. She would figure this out and come out on the other side okay.

"Don't be too hard on yourself. It's not every day you lose your dream apartment," Yvonne said as she studied the shelves with spools and spools of material. She tested the feel of the different textiles. "Next Act had these beautiful pieces in their front entrance, and I think I want to recreate them for our centerpieces."

"I really need to go one of these days," Jolene said.

The restaurant, Next Act, was where Yvonne proposed to Diana. It'd been the new "it" place to dine since it opened a year ago.

"I told you we saw Jason that night, right?"

"What?"

"Yeah, he was at the restaurant. We didn't talk or even make eye contact, but I saw him leave with some woman."

It was a weird moment because Jolene had been moving through her daily routines with Jason neatly tucked away for her subconscious to ponder. She'd talked herself out of taking that leap at the hospital, and now she found it hard to breathe thinking about him with another woman. Why was she like this? She had no right, no claim over him. She was the one who was still gallivanting around, trying to piece her life together. Her life might be at a standstill as she stressed about money and her career, but it didn't mean that he had to wait for her to figure it out.

"Oh, Jojo. I didn't mean to—"

Tears fell and ran down Jolene's chin without her notice. She swiped at her face harshly.

"It's fine. Oh my God. I'm such a mess. I've never cried so much in my life." Once Jolene managed to stop the unencumbered tears, she said, "Do you know he called me a coward?"

"You're not a coward, Jojo."

Jolene harrumphed. "I am, though. I've messed up a lot. I know that, and I've spent years trying to do better. Be better. And it's made me scared. I'm scared of messing up again, disappointing people, disappointing myself. Getting heartbroken again. But look at me"—she gestured to the general bubble around her—"I played it safe, and I still lost my job. Granted, I'm not responsible for that one, but I can't afford my beautiful apartment anymore, and I've pushed away a guy who's really amazing, Yvonne." Jolene took a big gulp of air. "Really, really amazing."

Yvonne nodded. There was no surprise, just simple confirmation. "So, what are you going to do about it?"

"I'm starting my own PR business," Jolene blurted out.

Just like when she told her sister, Jolene didn't feel the crushing, overwhelming feeling of dread and uncertainty that came when she previously thought about her business idea. Sure, there were still some nerves because she actually didn't know if this business venture would be a success. Most businesses failed, but she owed herself the risk.

"Okay, solid," Yvonne said. Jolene's declaration only seemed to only mildly throw her. "I expect to be at the top of the hiring pile. Now, what about Jason?"

It was a simple question. One she'd mulled over before but never could land on an answer that didn't make her stomach want to roll into itself. But she'd already shed tears in the store for all who monitored the security cameras to see. What were a few more minutes standing motionless and brooding, letting herself search for an answer?

In her mind, Jolene saw an image come together that was built in spite of her fears. It was beautiful, simple, and just out of reach. The butterflies that settled in her stomach urged her on.

She abruptly turned, walking to exit the aisle that had become too small and confined.

"How many more items on your list?" Jolene asked as she continued to walk the length of the aisle.

"Jolene."

She stopped only long enough to throw a reassuring smile over her shoulder at her friend and say, "I need to stop by the pet store before it closes."

Jason mumbled to himself, reciting the monologue he planned to deliver to Jolene. It included a robust apology, an explanation, and several possible solutions to her problems. He strode up to the entrance of her apartment complex, dialing her apartment number into the intercom. There was a chance that her schedule had changed, and she wasn't home on Saturday afternoons. He'd contemplated calling or texting her first to schedule some meeting after work. But he'd sat down to write a plan, and the plan took him to the florist where he'd purchased a large bouquet of gardenias, and as if momentum pulled him, he'd arrived at Jolene's apartment unannounced.

Only briefly while the intercom rang, did Jason think how awkward this might be.

After several rings he thought his trip would prove futile, but someone picked up on the sixth ring. "Hello?"

The high-pitched voice that came from the intercom was nothing like Jolene's voice.

"Sorry, is Jolene there?"

"Who?"

"Jolene Baxter?"

"Nah, you've got the wrong apartment."

Jason double-checked the numbers he'd entered.

"No, it's the right one."

"Sir, I don't know what to tell you. We've been here for two weeks already."

"All right, thank you. Sorry for bothering you."

Jolene didn't live here anymore. God, had she been evicted? The flowers now swung near his thigh as he walked and mentally drafted a Plan B. He was so caught up in the secondary plan that took shape that he arrived home without really recalling the actual journey. He fished his apartment keys from his pocket while trying not to drop his cell or Jolene's flowers. Preoccupied with these tasks, he failed to notice that Jolene herself had emerged from the corner of the vestibule of his apartment complex.

"Jason," she said.

He jumped and turned to where she stood. He wasn't wholly convinced that she stood before him. Maybe his guilty conscience sent an apparition to torture him. But she was all too real. She looked stunning, and she stood there holding a small box with no lid. He was too far from her to see what was inside. All he knew was that he wanted her to stay.

She gave the flowers that he held a quick look. "I'm sorry that I'm ambushing you on a Saturday. I thought you would be home—"

"Why, because I'm a homebody with no friends?" He meant the comment to sound lighthearted, but his still rapid heartbeat and lingering shock made the words sound more gruff and humorless than he intended.

She winced and ducked her head. "No, I texted your mom to see if you were running errands or at an event with her."

"You talk to my mom?"

"I've checked in on her periodically ever since the night at the hospital."

He knew that she did, but he liked hearing it from her.

She shook her head and said, "I know you might not want to see me or talk to me—"

Nope, that wasn't true. At that moment, he didn't want to see anyone but her.

"But I want to say—" She stopped and looked at him with a blank expression then at the ceiling. "Dammit," she said under her breath. "I had a whole speech, but I'm blanking."

"Do you want to come up and you can think about it while we walk?" he asked, reaching toward the door.

"I want to get this out right now."

He withdrew his hand and waited for her to continue.

"I know I'm not the bravest," she said.

Jason's heart skipped as he thought back to their argument the night at his place. "Jolene."

"No, it's okay."

He had to tell her about his involvement in her firing, but she withdrew what sat in the box before he could say anything else.

"Is that a clownfish?" Jason asked.

A single clownfish swam in circles around the bowl that Jolene revealed. The bottom of the bowl held multicolored rocks and an anemone ornament had been wedged into it. He didn't say anything, a little stunned. He struggled to decipher the meaning. He knew he'd been staring at the fish too long when Jolene cleared her throat.

"What I'm trying to say is, like the clownfish and anemone, we just work. We're people with different temperaments and approaches to life, but you inspire me to be bold, thoughtful, and indulge my feelings. And that's what I'm doing now." She tensed up a bit before saying, "I want to be with you."

Jason shut his eyes slowly to revel in the specifics of the moment like the shivers skipping up his spine. It was enough, but she continued to talk.

"I don't want it to be casual. I want it to be as serious as you are about having the right pan or pot to cook with or as serious as you are about your lists. That is, if you're willing to, if I haven't completely missed my chance—"

Jason could hear every beautiful word she said, but the blood rushing in his ears made him feel like she was far away. She obviously didn't know the details of her termination. She wouldn't be saying these things if she did.

"I need to tell you something before you continue." He resisted the need to take a hold of her hands.

She looked at the flowers again, and the vulnerability that he'd seen in her eyes moments ago, dulled as if she braced herself for what Jason had to say. And in that moment, he hated himself even more.

"Are you dating someone else?" she asked, her voice flat but the tension around her mouth betrayed her calm.

"No. It's nothing like that. It's… I'm the reason you got fired. I made a comment about Mark to his father, and it can't be a coincidence you lost your job right after. And I'm so sorry, Jolene. If I could take it back, I would. But I'll do whatever I need to do to help you get through this, whether that's pursuing legal channels, finding a better job, or even starting that business you dream about." He ended his very fast, very loud apology by presenting the flowers he'd bought for her. He expected to see shock or anger emanating from her, but not what he actually saw. Relief.

"You knew?" he asked.

She nodded. "Mark threw the fact in my face." She released a little laugh that sounded tinny to his ears.

Jason shook his head, trying to absorb her reaction. "You're not angry?"

She let out a laugh that was more like hers. "No. I've dumped that at the feet of the people actually responsible. All I have left for you is love."

His eyebrows shot up. Her eyes widened. All the sirens were going off in Jason's head that Jolene loved him. That's what she meant, right? He abandoned the flowers on the ground, grabbed the fish bowl, and carefully placed it on the dirty carpet next to the flowers.

"I know we haven't really talked about that or articulated our expectations," she said, rambling.

But Jason caught her unawares when he kissed her. It was a sweet one that was more a brush of his lips against hers than anything else. "I love you," he said as he released her lips.

Her eyes remained closed. "You don't have to say that—"

Cutting her off once again, he went in for another kiss. This time the kiss wasn't sweet or tame. He wanted to get his fill of her, and that involved drawing her flush against him, exploring and appreciating her scent and taste.

He came up for air and again said, "I love you."

Her eyes were glassy and her lips pouty when she looked up into his face. "Shit, I love you too." She grasped his neck and brought his mouth down to hers.

His hands circled her waist, but they refused to be stilled as they jumped up and down her body, recalling her curves and softness. They needed to get inside now before they put on a show for the whole neighborhood.

"God, I've missed you," Jolene said. "I need you inside me." The sound of her voice echoed in the closed quarters, and Jason tried to find the keys he'd abandoned on the floor without breaking contact with Jolene.

However, a voice severed their moment. "I just need to sneak past ya real quick."

Jason turned toward the voice of his neighbor, Gus, a high school teacher if he remembered correctly. Jolene laughed while Jason had a fierce scowl etched on his face. His dick was hard, and the friction that Jolene's body created against it made him clench his teeth.

"I'm sorry," Jason managed to say. He picked Jolene up, to her squealing surprise, to make room for the man to get to the door.

Gus didn't make further eye contact with them and entered the building.

"You're going to get me evicted," Jason said into the curve of Jolene's neck.

"Okay, but can you fuck me before that happens?"

———

She was on top of him. Her head thrown back as his hands dug into the flesh on her hips. His grip steadied her as she moved leisurely up and down the length of his dick, but the slight pain that his hands caused also amplified the building pleasure.

There came a point when the slow movement wasn't enough, and he flipped her onto her back and increased his pace. She felt him stretch and fill her. The sounds of their bodies connecting and their labored breathing coiled around her, and she found herself smiling when her orgasm hit. He anchored her to him at her waist and made several hard thrusts until he too came on deep throaty moans and with her name on his lips.

She found her spot in his arms as they rested.

"We need to find a better spot for our fish," Jason said as he studied the fish swimming atop his dresser.

She loved that he called it "our fish." She snuggled deeper into the curve of his body.

"Yeah, lest we jostle it off the surface when we have sex and incur the vengeful spirit of PETA," she said.

"Also, the fish needs more than just that bowl. We'll have to get it a large tank, some rocks, a filter, and a protein skimmer. Oh, and maybe even a live anemone," Jason said.

Jolene stared at him. The pet store had actually refused to sell her the clownfish without a tank and other vital apparatuses. All the equipment sat in the backseat of her car.

"How do you even know that?" she asked.

Jason shrugged. "My high school biology teacher had a saltwater tank in the classroom. What are we going to name him?"

"We shouldn't be sentimental, right?" She knew her head placement distorted her voice, but didn't care.

"No, let's do something really sentimental and cheesy. I thought something along the lines of Rowena or—"

"Nope. We're not naming our fish after her. She hates us, remember?"

"Fine. Fine. We can think of something. He's not going anywhere."

It was with that statement that Jolene basked in the sudden understanding that Jason wasn't going anywhere either. *They* had time.

Epilogue

One year later

One of the things Jolene loved about summertime was that the sun seemed resistant to set. She and Jason had spent the afternoon at Anthony's college going-away party eating, dancing, and shedding a few tears. They'd just arrived home, and though she was exhausted, the extra daylight spurred her to take advantage and do some work.

As she removed her heels and shimmied out of her bra, she watched as Jason fed their fish, Gregory. The way his suit strained against his large shoulders as he stood in front of the aquarium made a familiar flutter ignite in Jolene's body. If he caught her staring at him, there would be no chance for her to complete the things she needed to do before Monday morning. She quickly slipped into the home office they shared in their two-bedroom apartment and replied to several emails.

"I swear it's in here somewhere," she mumbled after peeling herself away from the Bermuda Triangle that was her email's inbox, and riffled through her organized files.

When she found what she was looking for, she triumphantly held it the air.

She was about to turn off the lights in the home office and chill for the rest of the night, when she noticed a few of Jason's intimidating medical textbooks on the shelf were slightly crooked. One of them jutted out and another he'd replaced upside down. Jason probably had been in a hurry when he took them out because there was no way that he would've left them like this. Jolene pushed one to straighten it, but it refused to budge. She took the books out to investigate what kept them from settling into place and found a tiny, black velvet box. She knew what it was the moment she laid eyes on it and giddiness formed in the pit of her belly.

She shouldn't look at the ring, so at least her shock when he did finally propose could be somewhat genuine. She dismissed the thought because her fingers were already prying the box open. Jolene stifled a squeal as she gazed upon the most beautiful ring she'd ever seen with several diamonds that would catch the light at the right angle. It would be a welcomed nuisance as she got into the nitty gritty of last-minute touch-ups on her office space and executing the grand opening of her very own PR firm, BAX Public Relations.

"What're you doing?"

Jolene let out a yelp and spun around to meet Jason's amused expression. He still wore his outfit from the party and looked so handsome, whereas Jolene had already removed her bra and wrestled her curly hair into a topknot, but you wouldn't know it from the way Jason looked at her.

"Nothing"—Jolene shoved her hands behind her back and crushed the box between her hands—"I was just looking for a form I need to send to the interior designer."

He came right up close and circled his arms around her, closing his hands around hers. Then leaned forward until they were a breath apart. "You're such a bad liar."

"Yes."

He raised one eyebrow. "You relented so fast. Is this real life?"

"I hope it's real, and I wasn't agreeing with your statement. I'm agreeing to marry you."

A small smile tugged at the corner of his lips. "I haven't asked."

"Get on with it, then."

He laughed in a way where his eyes wrinkled and nose scrunched up, and she wanted to wrap herself in the sound.

"I had a proper proposal planned out," he said.

"Plans change."

She was half joking and didn't expect him to actually abandon his beautiful planned proposal, but he gave her a quick kiss on the cheek before getting down on one knee.

"Jason, I was kidding—"

He smiled at her but stayed where he was. "Jolene Tiffany Baxter—"

I don't have a bra on.

"Jason." Her heart actually pounded even though she knew what was about to happen.

"You bring brightness into my life with every moment you're in it. There isn't a day that I can go through on autopilot because I feel with you."

He grabbed the ring box from her hands, and she looked upon the ring that would now be hers.

"I love you, Jolene. I want to spend the rest of my life showing you how much. Will you marry me?"

She was crying. Not cute, dainty tears you could blot

away with the pad of your thumb, but huge globs of tears spilling from her eye sockets and drenching her chin.

"Yes. Yes. One hundred times yes."

He stood and did his best to wipe away her tears before kissing her in a way that wasn't earth-tilting or shattering but made her feel grounded; it defined the lines and brought everything into focus. She was more than ready to face life as long as he was by her side.

Thank you!

Thank you so much for picking up *Along for the Ride*. I hope it gave you everything you needed. Jolene and Jason's story was so much fun to write, and I plan to give you more stories with different characters very soon. Visit www.mimigracebooks.com for updates on upcoming books.

About the Author

Mimi Grace credits romance novels for turning her into a bookworm at twelve years old. It didn't matter if those stories included carriages or cowboys, she could be found past her bedtime getting lost in a couple's journey to happily-ever-after.

If you don't include mint chocolate chip ice cream and long-running reality TV shows, romance novels are where Mimi finds the most joy.

She wants to evoke that same feeling in others with diverse books that are sexy, fun, and delightful. Visit her online at www.mimigracebooks.com.

 twitter.com/mimigracebooks

 instagram.com/mimigracebooks